HUMANITY ITSELF WAS THE ONLY FLAW IN THEIR PERFECT WORLD!

The Society of Mechanists considered themselves the inevitable rulers of the universe. Man in his fumbling, stumbling race for survival could not hope to stand against an order baptized by the merciless creed of logic and infallibility. To the Meks the faithful gave everything, asked nothing.

But though Operator Four-four had given up his body, his name . . . within him existed the seed of memory. And even in the camp of a bitter enemy, Four-four discovered that there were eternal laws that no man-made world could change.

A stand-out science-fiction novel that will hurtle you into the gripping new dimensions of the future.

CAST OF CHARACTERS

ALAN LORD

He entered on a mission that demanded his body—and even his soul.

MAURINE BURTON

She held the means to plunder other people's minds.

KARL ANEIDO

Even after his last dying gasp, he was able to play a trump card.

ZERO

The heart and brain of the Meks, he saw a new perfection within his grasp.

NARLA CHARLETT

An operative who mixed the passion for life with the cold logic of conquest.

NINE-SEVEN

He made men out of putty and putty out of men.

The Transposed Man

DWIGHT V. SWAIN

WILDSIDE PRESS

www.wildsidepress.com

CHAPTER I

"NAME?"

"Robert Travis."

"Occupation?"

"Mining engineer."

"Place of residence?"

"Seventh Base, Jovian Development Unit, Ganymede."

"Reason for visiting Luna?"

"I'm checking on performance of the new Dahlmeyer units in the Mare Nubium fields. We're thinking of adapting them for use in our Trendart field on Ganymede."

"I see. . . ." The port inspector fumbled through my papers. "Where's your celemental analysis sheet?"

I shrugged. "What would I be doing with a cell-sheet? I'm a mining engineer, not a damn' bureaucrat."

The way I said it made it good for a laugh, but the inspector just pawed some more at my papers and did not even smile. "New regulation. Everyone's got to pass a cell-check now."

"But I've got clearance—"

"That don't matter. All routine clearances are canceled." The inspector handed back my papers, jerked a thumb over his shoulder. "Go to the last window. They'll fix you up with a sheet and check it."

I went on over to the window and waited while two men

in white coats shoved a Van Cize celloscope up against a sad-faced, middle-aged woman's spine.

Then she moved on, and it was my turn.

The younger of the two white-coats adjusted the filter against the back of my neck. I decided he looked half human. "What's the idea?"

He grinned. "Mek trouble. Some idiot picked up a rumor that the Society's sending an agent to Luna, so Security orders cell-sheets for everybody. Me, I think it's a waste of time. If the damn' Meks are running a man in, he'll be under his own name. But you can't tell Security that." He stripped the sheet out of the celloscope. "Wait here a minute. This won't take long."

He stepped across to the check-frame, and I leaned back against the wall.

The port looked just about the way that I remembered it. A little older, maybe; a little dirtier. That was all.

A couple of other *Aurora* passengers drifted up to the window to get cell-sheets. They looked nervous. So did the others, the long lines of men and women still waiting for the port inspectors to check their papers.

I hummed a little tune. I didn't have to feel nervous. No one could identify me as Alan Lord, Mek agent; he lay back at The Center in a nutritor unit. I was Robert Travis, mining engineer, come all the way from Ganymede to Luna on legitimate business that anyone could check.

At least, for now I was.

I rubbed my elbow past the neurotron taped flat to my ribs; ran my hand over the spare strapped against my belly. A wonderful little invention, the neurotron. Given that, and my pulsator, and my com-set, I could go anywhere. Anywhere!

Young white-coat came back. "Travis . . ."

I turned. "That's me."

"You're clear." He handed me the cell-sheet. "Go on over through that door to baggage inspection."

The sad-faced woman was ahead of me at the counter. A customs man had her stuff spread out all over the counter. An octagonal metal case about eight inches each way stood in the center of it. The inspector was tapping the case and shaking his head.

I caught the tail end of what he was saying: ". . . but it's FedGov property, and there's no way in this world or any other that I can let you keep it without a special release."

The woman's face was white as alsop leather. I could see her lower lip quiver. "But it's all I've got!" she choked. "My husband's dead, crashed there on Ceres, and one of the search crew brought me back this astronometer. He was holding it, they said—holding it . . ."

She broke off, digging her chin down against her chest, sobbing in that awful, agonizing, silent way some women have. Looking at her, I suddenly saw Maurine instead, that night so long ago, the night she'd cried.

Maurine . . . My throat drew tight.

The baggage man looked past the woman to me, brows furrowing, and spread his hands in a helpless gesture. "Lady, I'm sorry, believe me! But even if I let you take it, they'd catch it at the raybot."

A raybot!

I swung around, not too fast, searching for it.

It stood at the far end of the counter, close by the door, where every person who went out would have to pass it.

My neurotrons would get through all right. So would the pulsator. But the com-set . . .

"I'm sorry, lady," the baggage man said again. He was stuffing the woman's possessions back into the cases now. "Believe me, I'm sorry."

He picked up the astronometer and bent to put it underneath the counter.

I shot one quick glance around. No one was near; no one was watching. The woman still had her face hidden in her hands.

I slipped the pulsator—it was fitted into a writer case for camouflage purposes—out of my pocket and flipped the button. Before the baggage man could straighten, I leaned across the counter and touched the thing to his shoulder.

He gave a convulsive jerk and sprawled flat on his face on the floor. I vaulted the counter and dropped to my knees beside him, dragging one of the woman's blouses with me. Other customs men were turning, staring.

"His heart!" I clipped. "Quick! Get a doctor!"

Rolling the unconscious man over, I straightened his legs. That took me halfway under the counter—and under cover —back where the astronometer lay. Twisting open the adjustment panel, I shoved my com-set inside the case, then slapped the panel shut again and wadded the blouse around the bulky instrument.

Two customs men dragged my victim out into the open. I rose and skidded the astronometer across the counter, into the sad-faced woman's welter of possessions.

She stared at me blankly.

"He dropped it, Miss"—I glanced at her papers—"Mrs. Nordstrom. I hope it's not hurt."

Her blue eyes widened with sudden understanding. Hastily, she fitted the astronometer into one of her cases.

I turned to the nearest customs man. "This poor woman's

husband was just killed in a crash on Ceres. Can't you get
her out of here? He"—I nodded toward the prostrate inspector—"was helping her repack when he collapsed."

He glanced at the litter. "Sorry this had to happen, ma'am.
Sure, go ahead." He turned back to the man on the floor.

"Hasn't someone even gotten some water yet?" I demanded. "You people sure would have a hell of a time in a
mining camp!" I elbowed my way past the inspectors and
ran down the aisle behind the counter toward the raybot.

The switch was on the back, just as I remembered. I
brushed hard against it. It snapped off.

I turned around and ran back. "No water at this end.
Where in hell's the water?"

One of the customs men glowered at me. "What's it to
you, mister? And what are you doing behind this counter,
anyhow?"

I glared back. "If that's the way you feel about it—"

"That's just the way we feel about it! Get back on your
own side." The inspector's ears were pink. "Here! Where's
your baggage? I'll check it myself."

Out of the corner of my eye, I could see Mrs. Nordstrom
hesitate momentarily by the raybot, then step onto the scanner platform, luggage in hand.

Nothing happened.

Quickly, she went on out the street door.

"Well, you, what about it?" the customs man grunted.
"Can't you spot your stuff?"

I glanced down at the man who'd taken the jolt from my
pulsator.

His mouth opened . . . closed . . . opened again. Noisily,
he sucked in air.

Five more minutes and he'd feel fit as ever. I grinned.

"Well?" It was Old Sorehead again.

"Right there, behind your man." I pointed to Robert Travis' bags. "The twin chronel jobs. . . ."

CHAPTER II

MY CONTACT'S name was Raines, John Raines. I checked in at one of the big port hostels—Travis had made reservations —and called his number on the voco.

"Hello . . ." It was a wary, greasy sort of voice.

"Is this Mr. Raines?"

"Yes. But who—"

"This is Robert Travis, Mr. Raines. I'm with Jovian Development, here on business. Our Mr. Azlon told me I'd find it worth my while to talk over some of the technical details with you."

"Azlon? Azlon?"

"A-z-l-o-n." I let it hang for just an instant. "Z, as in zero."

"Oh!"

"I'm at Port Hostel Number Three," I said. "Room six-one-nine. I've got to head out for the Mare Nubium fields on the first carrier next cycle, so it would help if we could get together right away."

"Oh . . ." Raines' voice wasn't quite so slick and greasy now. He sounded like a man trying to fumble his way out of a spot he didn't like.

"Why don't you come up for a drink or two, Mr. Raines?

No need for our talk to be dry, even if it is technical,"
I suggested.

"Why . . . uh . . ."

"Good." I clipped it short, not waiting for excuses. "You
know how Mr. Azlon is. Neither of us would ever hear the
last of it if we didn't get together."

"Of—of course . . ."

"Right away, then. I'll be waiting."

I thumbed the button down smartly to click a good, sharp
period to the conversation, then turned to the directory hanging on the voco rack and leafed through it till I came to
Nordstrom, Helmar. The address was the same as that on
the sad-faced woman's papers—close to the port, in one of
the astrogation personnel units.

I dialed the number. After a moment a woman's voice
answered: a sad voice, a voice with tears in it.

I clicked the button without speaking, and got up and
went over to the window. It was the usual plasticon, cheap
and beginning to warp, but with a Schweidler bipolaroid
selecter so that you could cut off the outside light when
you wanted to go to sleep—a handy thing on a satellite like
Luna, where the days seemed to last forever.

Below me, autotrans spun along the ramp-spanned streets
that sliced between the buildings' dull spun-doloid walls like
lines in some complicated geometric problem. Beyond the
buildings, outside the transparent shell that held the artificial
atmosphere, the port spread in a gray-brown desert plain
spiked with ramped silver spaceships. Far off I could see
the shimmering green ripples that were the hydroponic
tubes. And overhead . . .

I looked up.

Terra hung there . . . Terra, my homeland, the great

green ball that forever wheeled slowly in Luna's sky. Maurine Dorsett's homeland, too. Terra and Maurine—they were linked together deep inside me, down where it hurt. Bleakly, I wondered if I'd ever see either of them again.

I was glad when the buzzer rang.

The man at the door looked as greasy as his voice. He was short, fat; he wore a sickly smile that seemed pasted on.

"I—I'm Raines . . ." He kept dodging my eyes.

"I'm Travis." I stepped out of the way so he could come in and closed the door behind him. "Sit down. Have a drink."

He juggled the glass as if it were hot instead of cold. He didn't speak.

I said, "We might as well get to the point fast, Raines. The Center sent me here to check on two things: Aneido's visit, and the shorties."

For the first time, his eyes came up. "The shorties?"

"We call them that." I worked on my drink. "Our laboratories have a shielding system. It's based on the fact that the human mind is actually an electrical device, a sort of organic computer and selector."

"Yes."

"Our shield is electrical, too. It's keyed to the same frequency as the human brain. Whenever anyone who's not insulated wanders into its field, it throws out tracer charges —not strong enough to kill, but so heavy that they short-circuit the brain synapses.'

"Permanently?"

"Permanently."

Raines shuddered.

"It's too bad," I clipped. "Zero doesn't like it a bit better than you do. But we've got to keep our laboratories secret. The Society's work is more important than snooping strays. If you don't believe that, you've got no business being a Mechanist."

Raines stared down at his glass, not speaking. His face had taken on a grayish tone, and tiny, greasy globules were appearing along the creases around his mouth and in the puffy flesh below his eyes.

"The important thing," I hammered, "is that those short-circuits survive. That's all right. Their minds are blanks. They can't give us away. Most of them are picked up by the authorities, sooner or later. So, for years, the FedGov's psych boys have beaten their brains to a pulp trying to figure out what's happened to the shorties, but they've never gotten to first base."

"Then what—" Raines fumbled.

I leaned forward. "Something's happened," I clipped, "something the Society needs to know about fast. Out of a clear blue sky, orders have been sent down to all FedGov Security units to channel all shorties direct to the Humanics Research laboratories here on Luna." I gulped the rest of my drink, set down my glass. "What about it, Raines? You're with Humanics Research; that's why The Center decided to make you my contact. What's happening to those shorties?"

Raines squirmed and ran one pudgy hand around the back of his fat neck. "That—that's a secret project. . . ."

"Are you going to quote me security rules?" I came up fast, crowding in close to him. "Believe me, Raines, that's not what Zero would think was a satisfactory excuse."

"But I don't know. It's not my project!" His voice had gone shrill. He cringed as far back in the chair as he could get. Sweat trickled out of the short hair along his ear and slid down his jaw. "Electro-neural Testing handles all that work. Doctor Burton's in charge."

"And you know this Burton?"

"Why . . . uh, yes; of course."

"All right." I stepped back and sat down again. "Now, about the other reason I came here: Aneido's visit."

"You mean . . . *General* Aneido? The Security chief?"

"Who else?"

"I—I didn't even know he was here."

"But you know where he'd be if he was here, don't you? The Security offices, the quarters where they put up visiting power piles?"

"Yes." Raines dragged out a rumpled handkerchief and wiped the sweat from his chin. "They—they keep an apartment over in the big Quiverna unit. We've already got a plant next door—a fellow named Heffner who's on the budget council."

"Good." I got up and put on my coat. "It's time we got to work, Raines. First, I want to meet this Burton."

Raines set down his glass. It rattled on the table.

"Come on!" I prodded.

He still didn't get up. I let the silence drag, waiting.

He shifted and wiped his forehead. "Mr. Travis . . ."

I didn't answer.

"Mr. Travis, you don't realize what you're asking!" He burbled the words, moving his hands in helpless, pawing gestures too small for the bulk of him. "What excuse could I make for introducing you to Doctor Burton? And what good would it do? She wouldn't tell you anything—"

I cut him short: "She?"

"Dr. Burton is . . . a woman."

I waited some more.

"Besides . . . Security knows a Somex agent's coming. They're even making cell-checks! And if they should catch you—after I'd introduced you . . . I shouldn't even be here now."

Just watching him did things to my stomach. I looked away, off out the window, and touched the pulsator in my pocket. "Don't worry. Nobody's going to catch me."

"But—"

I swung around. "Don't worry, I said. I've changed my mind. I'm not even going to ask you to go with me."

"Mr. Travis—" He struggled up out of the chair, and his face was like sunrise in Yogorbo. "Oh, I can't tell you how much I appreciate this, Mr. Travis . . ."

"Forget it," I said. "I understand."

Flipping the pulsator button, I went with him to the door. He reached for the knob. I touched the pulsator to the back of his neck. He straightened spasmodically and half turned. His mouth was gaping, his eyes already glazed.

I caught him under the arms before he could fall, dragged him to the bed and heaved him up onto it, face down. Opening my shirt, I unstrapped the spare neurotron from its place against my—or rather, Travis'—belly, got out the scalpel blade, and slit the skin behind each of Raines' ears. They were only half-inch cuts, following the edge of the hair over the bulging upper ridge of bone. Raines didn't even stir.

The electrodes were paper thin. I worked them into the slits carefully, one on each side, making sure that they were seated solidly against the bone before I rubbed on the skinseal to close the cuts. By the time I had finished, not even a dermatologist could have detected anything amiss without a glass.

Next, I peeled up Raines' coat and shirt along his side,

taped the neurotron itself into place, and tested the adjustment.

Raines moved uneasily. I began to pick up the hazy, disconnected fragments of thought that sometimes seep through from a host's own mind.

Lying down on the bed beside him, I slid the activator contact over. There was a moment of black chaos. I couldn't see nor hear nor speak. Then it faded, and I had the usual queer feeling of being split two ways. With an effort, I fumbled the activator contact on the Travis neurotron to the open position. The split feeling vanished. Stiffly, I rolled over and sat up.

Robert Travis lay prone on the bed beside me. He was breathing a trifle raggedly; that was all. Otherwise, he looked exactly the same as he had the first tme I'd seen him, that night on Mars. I laughed, and wished I could see his face when he woke up and found himself already in a port hostel on Luna, with the whole trip in from Mars a blank.

Getting up, I went over to the mirror, took stock of my new personality and decided that I didn't like John Raines any better from the inside than from without.

The clock above the door said this cycle was nearly half gone. Stripping, I went into the light-bath and tried to beam away the worst of Raines'—my own, now—greasy look, then came out and dressed again.

The clothes were like rags; even the coat had a scarecrow drape. I tried to shrug it into some sort of shape, but a stiffness through the shoulders balked me.

I took the coat off again and worked the fabric between my hands. The stiffness lay between outer shell and lining. The meld wouldn't give, so I slashed a three-inch gash in the lining just below the collar.

The stiffness took the form of three narrow, flexible strips of what appeared to be plastic. One, blue and about six inches long, had been melded to the coat-fabric horizontally. The other two strips were green and twins, each nearly a foot in length. One of them dangled down vertically from either end of the blue cross-bar.

When I looked up, the clock said another half-hour had passed. Time was running out. I put the coat back on, retrieved my pulsator and spare neurotron from Robert Travis, and left the hostel.

CHAPTER III

THE BUILDING directory at Humanics Research said John Raines had an office in Wing G. So did Doctor Burton. I tried Raines' office first.

The door was unlocked. A tall, thin, stoop-shouldered girl stood by a microfile cabinet just inside, flipping a record reel through the reader.

I nodded to her, not pausing, and headed for the bigger of the room's two desks. When I turned to sit down, I found she had closed the door and was standing with her back against it, smiling.

Fumbling at the papers on the desk, I smiled back.

She shot me a kittenish, low-lashed look. "John . . ." Her

fingers picked nervously at the belt of her cheap purple veldrene dress.

I opened a desk drawer and poked at the jumble inside. "Yes?"

"You . . . forgot something, John."

"Well . . ."

"John, are you angry with me?" Her smile vanished, leaving her pallid and hollow-eyed. She came toward me with uneven steps. "What is it? What's wrong?"

"Nothing. Nothing at all." I closed the drawer and bent over the papers.

"Yes. There is." She clutched my shoulder. "Tell me, John. Tell me!"

I began to sweat. "Look, I'm just tired . . ." I tried to push her away.

"John—" She pawed at me. "John, is it that Burton woman? Has she been making more trouble?"

I started. "Burton—"

"John, have you been seeing her again?"

"No, no, no—"

"John, you have! You're still in love with her!"

I struggled up from the chair. "Are you crazy? Once and for all, leave me alone!"

"No, John! No . . ." She clawed at me, smearing me with clammy, ill-aimed kisses. Her frizzed hair got in my eyes and nose, and I bumped my chin on her scrawny collarbone. "I love you, John! I've given you everything. You can't expect me to just stand by quietly while you run off after another woman—"

The girl's voice rose shrilly. She began to sob.

I shot a quick glance toward the door. I could feel the sweat trickling down my back. "Please . . ." Awkwardly, I put my arms around the creature and smoothed her hair. "Look, dearest, I'm just tired, I tell you. I've got a lot on my mind . . . things to do before the end of the cycle . . ."

Sniffling, she wriggled against me.

I patted her shoulder. "Now, darling, I really have got to go."

She twisted, peered at me out of watery eyes. "But to-night—"

"Don't worry. I'll see you," I broke in hurriedly. "I'll only be gone a little while."

Her lower lip was still quivering. "All right, John. But—but kiss me first."

It was a moist kiss and too prolonged.

I went out into the corridor again, swabbing the sweat from my face with John Raines' soggy handkerchief and scrubbing my mouth with the back of my hand.

Doctor Burton's office was locked. I knocked.

There was a moment's pause, then muffled footsteps. The door opened. A man stared out at me. He was about thirty-five, tall, well-built, almost too good looking.

I said, "I want to see Doctor Burton."

His jaw set. "The question is, does she want to see you." He turned his head, spoke over his shoulder: "Maurine, the fat boy's here again. Do you want me to let him in?"

A woman exclaimed, "What?" and then, "No; I'll come there, Fred."

I frowned and moved back a little. I had a strange feeling I'd heard that voice somewhere before. Again, there was the sound of footsteps—quicker, this time; lighter. The man stepped out of the way. A woman appeared beside him in the doorway. I caught my breath.

It was Maurine Dorsett. The years had hardly touched her.

Transformed from girl into woman, she still stood poised and
slender. The gesture with which she smoothed and shaped
the dark hair that swept down to the nape of her neck in a
loose coil was as familiar as yesterday.

"Well?" Faint scorn tinged her tone, her glance. The cool,
intelligent eyes measured me as if I were a laboratory specimen.

I groped. "I . . . had an inquiry on your project—"

The man beside Maurine snorted. "You mean, you thought
you might find her alone this close to the end of the cycle."

She laid a slim, silencing hand on his arm.

"All inquiries regarding my project go through Security,
Mr. Raines. You know that." Her voice was as cool as her
eyes.

I fumbled, ran a hand over the back of my neck. "I—I'm
sorry . . ."

"You'll be a lot more than sorry if I catch you bothering
Doctor Burton again!" the man in the doorway lashed. He
took a quick step forward and caught me by my coat-front.
He pushed his face down close to mine. "Get this, Raines:
The next time I find you sneaking around here I'll take care
of you myself!"

"Fred!" Maurine's voice cut like a whip.

His handsome face turning sullen, the man let go of me.

Maurine said, "Mr. Raines, I believe that by now it should
be plain to anyone that I don't care to have anything further
to do with you. If you actually have business that needs my
personal attention, I'd much prefer that we transact it in
writing, through channels."

She turned, went back into the office. The man shot me a
final, hate-dripping glance and followed. The door swung
shut noisily—almost a slam. I stared at the closed door for a

long moment. Then I swung around and walked off down the corridor. I kept on going till I was out of the Humanics Research building.

There was an autotran port across the street. I got into the first empty and ran the tracer over the shortest route to the astrogation personnel unit listed as the home of *Nordstrom, Helmar*.

Stepping into the unit manager's office, I borrowed writer, paper and envelope from the girl on duty and scribbled, *Your husband loaned me this a long time ago* on the paper. No signature. Folding the note around a fifty-credit bill, I sealed it in the envelope and addressed it to Mrs. Nordstrom. Then I dialed her number on the voco.

It was four rings before she said hello. She sounded as if she had been crying.

I said, "This is the unit manager's office, Mrs. Nordstrom. Could you drop down for a moment? Something's developed that we need to discuss with you."

She hesitated for a moment. Then in a weary voice she said, "Of course."

"Thank you." I hung up, gave the envelope to the girl, and left the office.

The Nordstrom apartment was on the third level. As soon as I was out of view from the unit office, I doubled over to the lift and rode on up. Down the corridor, Mrs. Nordstrom was just closing her door. I walked past her with no sign of recognition.

She disappeared into the lift. I came back and went to work on her door's tab-lock. In thirty seconds the bolt clicked back. I stepped inside the apartment and closed and locked the door.

The astronometer stood on a small, ornate Venusian lorsch

table in one corner of the living room. A sepia-toned, tri-dimensional kalatograph of a heavy-faced man wearing a space officer's cap hung in the wall angle above and behind it.

I twisted open the adjustment panel, dragged out my com-set, closed the panel, and went out the back door of the apartment just as Mrs. Nordstrom unlocked the front.

Out in the street once more, I caught another autotran, ran the finder over a long, eratically patterned route, then tapped out my signal on the com-set's call button.

The amplifier buzzed. "Identify yourself," a curt male voice commanded.

I leaned back in my seat and held the grillwork close to my mouth. "Four-to-the-fourth-power."

"Pass, four-four."

I said, "Top emergency. Let me talk to Zero."

"To Zero—" The voice from the amplifier sounded startled. "You know that's impossible. I'm authorized—"

"To hell with your authorization," I clipped. "I want Zero. This is Project X business."

There was more sputtering and muttering from the duty man, fading away to silence. Then another circuit clicked in, and Zero's voice crackled—incisive, peremptory. "Four-four, what's the trouble?"

I said, "My contact man fizzled out. I had to take him over with the neurotron."

"With the neurotron . . ." Zero's tones grew wintry. "It's a violation of orders to take over a member, Four-four. You know that."

"Even if he's a double agent?"

"A double agent!"

"It's happened before."

"But that contact . . ." Zero's voice faded for a moment, then came back hard and clipped. "You've got definite evidence he's been reached by Security?"

"I don't know," I admitted. "Not for sure. But he had the shakes beyond all reason, and I find he's been tangled up with at least two women."

"Who are they?"

"One's his secretary—a messy business. The other may be the key to this whole project. She's—"

"No names!"

I grunted. "Don't worry. I know the rules."

"Sometimes I wonder." The amplifier droned, wordless, for an instant. "Which segment of the project is she related to, A or B?"

"A. I haven't had time to get anything first-hand on B."

"And your contact—"

"He was A, too."

"Then that's all your proof against him? Just what you've mentioned?" The frost was creeping back into Zero's voice.

"Not quite." I told him about the plastic strips melded into Raines' coat, describing them in detail.

"They could be the focal point for some new kind of finder the Security labs have developed. . . ." Zero sounded thoughtful. "You'd better bring that coat in when you come. Our com-men may be able to make something of it. Meanwhile"—more chill—"pay a little attention to regulations, Four-four. You're good; you're efficient. I'm the first to admit. But you've got a headstrong streak, and we both know it. You didn't have to take your contact man over with the neurotron to handle this."

I didn't say anything.

"Is there anything else?" Zero demanded.

"Yes."

"Well?"

I shifted, drew in a quick breath. "I want to be relieved of my assignment."

"What?" The amplifier squawked under the volume climb. "What nonsense—"

I muffled the amplifier with my palm. "No nonsense. I'm making a formal request for relief. For personal reasons."

For a few seconds the only sound coming over the com-set was the faint whisper of heavy breathing. Then Zero said, "Request denied." The temperature had dropped to match his title.

I kept quiet.

Zero said icily, "The Society of Mechanists requires that its members accept strict discipline, Four-four. For an agent on a mission as vital as Project X, the standards are ten, a hundred, a thousand times as rigorous as they are for an ordinary worker."

I waited some more.

"Just what are these overwhelming personal reasons that force you to ask to abandon your job, Four-four?"

I said, "They're personal."

"Personal . . ." The edge on Zero's voice suddenly wasn't quite so sharp. "How long have I known you, Four-four?"

"Ten years."

"Ten years . . ." He made it sound like a long, long time. "Ten years, Four-four. And in all that period, you've never once tried to hold back anything from me."

I didn't answer.

"Ten years . . . and you say a woman may be the key to this whole project."

I shifted on the autotran's seat. My hand was suddenly

sweaty on the com-set. I scrubbed it dry against my pant-
leg.

"There was a woman for you once, wasn't there, back a
dozen years ago, before I even knew you?" A pause. "Where
is she now, Four-four? Could she be . . . on Luna?"

"Shut up!" I smashed my fist down on the com-set's grillwork. "A man's human, damn you! Just leave it the way I
said it! I'm asking to be relieved from this assignment—"

"—for personal reasons." The ice was all gone now. Zero
sounded old and tired. "Believe me, Four-four, I understand."

"Then—"

"No." I could almost see him shake his head. "You say a
man's human, Four-four. But you're not a man. You're a
Mechanist. The Society's work means more than you, more
than your feelings. We can't afford to let this project fail.
You'll have to go ahead according to plan."

"But—"

"Request denied."

The amplifier clicked off.

CHAPTER IV

THEY called the place the Moon Room. A replica of Luna,
as seen from Earth, hung like a dim gold crescent against
the deep blue of the artificial sky. Stars twinkled, and an
aromador brought subtle fragrances of forests and streams
and wind-swept hills. A thread of faint, languorous melody
sighed and rippled on the climatizer's gentle breeze.

I gulped a vidal, then ordered spiked loin of rossa, seared

in lorsch, with doralines from Mars and a salad of Ionian
tabbat stalks.

It was good food. The rossa measured a full two inches
thick, deep pink straight through, the fibers so tender from
the infradation that my fork sliced them like a knife. The
quince-tinted tabbat stalks—not one longer than a tarosette
—had been gathered at the peak of their delicate flavor. I ate
slowly, savoring every mouthful.

Afterward, there was thick Venusian ronhnei coffee, then
more vidal. This time I didn't gulp it.

The cycle was over now. The long, dim room began to fill
with other patrons, couples mostly. I leaned back, rolling the
tear-shaped glass between my hands, watching idly as the
diners took their places.

A woman, alone, paused momentarily at the threshold. She
was taller than most, sleek-lined and with her hair swept up
and around in a style I'd never seen before. Stepping inside
quickly, out of the opener beam, she disappeared into the
shadows. The chromoid street door whispered shut behind
her.

I caught the waiter's eye and tapped my empty glass. He
nodded and headed for the bar. A hand touched my elbow.
I came around with a jerk. The tear-drop glass rang against
the table.

"Oh, did I startle you, darling? I'm sorry."

It was the woman—girl, rather, I saw now—with the unique
coiffure, the one who'd paused in the doorway. She sat down
beside me without waiting for an invitation.

Seeing her at closer range, I understood why she'd picked
such an unusual style for her hair. Even in the dimness, it
shone and rippled—thick, rich, tawny.

She smiled at me and moved her chair around a little

closer. "Please try to forgive me, dear; I know I'm late. But they had a sale on hair brooches at a little place over near my unit, and you know how I love that kind of thing. Just look at the one I picked—the sets are real fire rubies!"

She slipped a clip out of her hair and handed it to me.

The pattern was one of interlinked zeros.

"Nice," I said. I pushed back my chair. "Shall we go?"

"Oh, can't I have just one vidal?" The girl was half smiling, half pouting. Even pouting, she was pretty. The waiter picked that moment to come back. I gave the girl the vidal.

She sipped it slowly, still smiling. There was something about her smile, something that reminded me of Maurine. I said, "Hurry up. We're late already."

She drained the glass without a word and rose in one smooth, graceful motion. We left the Moon Room.

The street outside was narrow. It ran between buildings so tall that down here at ground level we were in deep shadow, crushed down by the sheer bulk of looming spundoloid walls. Even the air seemed heavy.

The girl tilted her head. "Which way?" Her eyes were wide, and the corners of her mouth twitched as if she were having a hard time trying not to laugh.

"To the Quiverna," I said.

She turned right.

I fell in beside her. "Why did you come? Why not Heffner?"

"He didn't want to take the chance. He's on the budget council."

"Then why send anyone? I could have found his place without a guide."

She shot me a sidewise glance. "Not at the Quiverna."

"You mean—"

"You don't just walk into the Quiverna. It's for important people only. You have to be with someone who lives there to get in."

I nodded. "I see." We walked on a little further.

The girl's steps lagged. She gave me another low-lashed, sidewise look. "They . . . didn't tell me anything about you, who you were, why it was so important for you to get to Mr. Heffner's apartment."

"That's good."

She pursed her lips. "What *is* your name, anyhow?"

I threw her a stony look. "The Society's first security rule is that members must never reveal their names to other members. You know that."

She made a face at me. "I'll call you 'Hey-you,' then."

"I didn't mean—"

She veered sharply, pulling me toward a shop window. "Oh, look at that rexolite gown! Isn't it lovely?"

I choked. "All rexolite gowns are lovely. That's why they cost so much. But sometimes other things can be important, too. Right now, I need to get into the Quiverna."

"Of course . . . Mr. Hey-you."

I dragged her bodily away from the window.

She hung on my arm, laughing, head back, tawny hair ashimmer. "Oh, aren't the stars beautiful? Do you think we'll ever reach them? Do you? Even with the new Karapesh drive, they're so far away. . . ."

"I ought to cut your throat on a Karapesh drive," I snarled. "Come on!"

"But it's so early. We could look at the stars—"

"Damn the stars."

We reached the Quiverna's pretentious vitraline-and-chromoid entrance. Still giggling, the girl slipped her card into the tab-lock of the outer door. Noiselessly, it swung open.

The area beyond was bare, brightly lighted. A voice from nowhere said, "Good evening, Miss Cherritt. You have a guest?"

"Yes." She turned to smile at me, eyes dancing. "He's Mister—"

"Raines," I cut in hastily. "John Raines. Humanics Research unit."

"Of course, Mr. Raines." The voice was ever so polite. "Will you please step over to the celloscope for registration? Security requires us to file a check-sheet on all visitors."

As the voice spoke, a panel in the wall to my left slid back, revealing a Van Cize unit's gaping lens.

I planted the back of my neck against it.

"Thank you very much, Mr. Raines. Just ring the bell inside when you're ready to leave."

A bolt clicked faintly. The inner door opened. I followed the Cherritt girl to the lift.

"Seventh level . . . Mr. Hey-you."

I swore under my breath.

"This way, Mr. Hey-you. Mr. Heffner's apartment is seven-three-three."

We walked down a long, silent corridor carpeted in dark rose veldrene to a door marked 733.

The girl reached for the buzzer. I knocked her hand down. She stepped back quickly, the laughter dying in her eyes.

I said, "You're going home now."

"But Mr. Heffner—"

"To hell with Mr. Heffner!" I caught her wrist. "You think this is just a game, don't you? It's fun, exciting. I thought so, too, once."

Her lips moved. "You're . . . hurting . . ." The color had begun to drain from her face.

"Good!" I lashed savagely. "Maybe it'll help you to remember what I'm telling you." I twisted till her knees buckled and she swayed against me—head back, eyes closed, mouth working. "Listen! You're human. You like to laugh, to have fun. Maybe some day you'll even fall in love. But Mechanists aren't human. Mechanists are machines that are alive, tearing themselves to pieces while Security stands by and throws rocks in among the gear wheels. They've forgotten how to laugh, and fun is something other people talk about, and love is an obsolete word describing electro-chemical reactions in an organic test tube."

I ran out of words and shoved her away from me so hard she tripped and caromed off the wall, down onto the dark rose veldrene carpeting.

"Go home, you little fool! Get out while you've still got the chance! Go back to your thousand-credit Quiverna apartment and forget you ever heard of such an outfit as the Society of Mechanists!"

I stood there—fists clenched, breathing hard—while she dragged herself up, eyes fearful and uncertain. Her mouth opened as if to speak, then closed again. Without a word, she turned and limped off down the hall. For a moment before she vanished, I thought I could hear her crying.

I jabbed the buzzer.

The door opened a crack. A black eye peered out at me. "Heffner?"

The crack widened. A wizened face came into view, skin parchment sallow. The nervous black eyes looked past me, flicking glances up and down the hall.

"She's gone," I clipped. "I sent her home. This isn't public business."

"Oh." It was a croak, more than a word. The door swung back the rest of the way. I stepped inside.

Heffner closed the door after me. He was a little man, bent and spindle-thin. His features were pinched, his skull balding. His fingers trembled so much he had trouble with the bolt. "I—I'm not used to this kind of business. I never expected—"

"You never expected to have to deliver, is that it?" I swung round and looked over the room, with its paradone and chromoid and foamex—all the accouterments of luxury. "You figured the Society would go on helping you pay for this just as a worthy charity that was your due as a member of the budget council."

Heffner bumped against a low stand of inlaid azure chromoid. His eyes sparked. "Young man—"

I kept on prodding: "Did you think our work was all just talk, Mr. Heffner? Or were you just stupid?"

I could see his lips draw thin. He'd stopped trembling.

I said, "No one ever thinks his own day is really going to come, when he joins the Society. Only now yours is here, so let's get on with it."

"What do you want?" He was biting off his words now.

"A look at the apartment next to this one—the one Security holds for special visitors."

He nodded stiffly. "This way."

I followed him to another door. He unlocked it, and we passed into a bedroom.

He touched the left wall. "Their living room is just beyond this. And we've installed a perceptoscope . . ."

"Good." I waited while he wheeled the bulky case out of a closet. "You can go back in the other room now."

His nostrils flared angrily. Pivoting, he stalked out, leaving me alone.

I closed the door behind him, then aligned the percepto-scope's scanner against the wall and flipped the switch. Slowly, as the tubes warmed, the scope's screen began to glow. A dim image took form.

Humming, I adjusted the focusing dials. The image sharp-ened, till it was as if I were looking through a window into the adjoining room. Save for details, the place duplicated the luxury of Heffner's broad parlor: tinted chromoid fur-nishings made less bleak by the sparkle of paradone insets, veldrene carpeting and Nacromean velvet drapes—a decor that combined triangularity with sleek Modarc curves.

While I watched, a heavy-set, middle-aged man in formal FedGov uniform moved into the scope-screen's frame. He walked like a bear. His cuffs bore the triple planets of a general officer, while his shoulder-patch carried the silver shield and black dagger of the Security Service.

Pausing in the middle of the room, he glanced toward a clock on a stand nearby. It brought his head round. I saw his face. It was Aneido—Aneido himself, General Karl Aneido, chief of the whole FedGov security system.

I stopped humming. My fingers were suddenly slippery on the focusing dials. Aneido belched. Frowning at the clock, he ran thick fingers through a mass of wiry black hair. With infinite care, I pin-pointed the focus.

The general lumbered over to a built-in microbook case, ran a blunt thumb across the backs of the reel-cartons on the top shelf, finally pulled one out. Prodding a foamex chair closer to the reader, he sat down with a jounce, snapped the reel into place, threaded the film and clicked the first frame onto the screen of the reader.

Now the broad shoulders slumped a trifle. The lines that set off the thick lips and heavy jaw looked less like chiseled granite. Then, abruptly, his head came up. Eyes no longer sleepy, he stared across the room at some point outside the scope-screen's frame.

Hurriedly, I snapped on the audio unit. Aneido surged up from his chair and lumbered out of view. The audio picked up the click of a door latch. A man's voice said, "My dear doctor! I'm so glad you found time to come."

The words were pleasant enough, but the voice held iron undertones. There was no answer; only the sound of the door closing.

Aneido moved back onto the scope-screen. "Over here, please, Doctor. We have so much to talk about." He chuckled.

A woman stepped into the frame, a trimly slender woman with dark hair. It was Maurine. There was no reading her expression. Still without a word, she crossed to the chair Aneido indicated and sat down, smoothing the skirt of her dark suit across her knees.

Aneido said, "We'll talk in just a moment. Wait. . . ."

He disappeared again, then came back with a crackle-finish black metal case about a foot square and six inches thick. Dropping into the foamex chair, he opened a panel in the front of the box. Inside was a single switch. Maurine looked at the case, then at Aneido. I could see her brows draw together just a fraction.

Aneido laughed. "No need to look so puzzled, my dear. It's just that this matter is so important we can't afford to take chances on a leak. This little device"—he ran a blunt thumb along the black case—"insures us against eavesdroppers."

"Eavesdroppers?" It was the first time Maurine had spoken. There was a tenseness in her voice.

"A very dangerous eavesdropper, Doctor," Aneido nodded. He leaned forward. The pupils of his eyes seemed to dilate. "Tell me, please: what do the numbers four-four mean to you?"

I stood stock still.

"Four-four?" Maurine traced patterns on the purse in her lap with a gloved forefinger. "I'm afraid it doesn't mean anything to me, General."

"I'm very glad to hear you say that, Doctor. Because four-four is the Somex numerical designation for the man who's the top Mek secret agent." Aneido moved in his seat. His head seemed to sink down between the heavy shoulders. "He's on Luna now."

"On Luna?" Maurine's head lifted. "But . . . I thought you'd instituted a cell-check."

"Ah, the cell-check. . . ." The general chuckled mirthlessly. "Never underestimate an adversary, my dear. This man is daring and truly clever. He has a powerful organization behind him. We think he slipped through inspection in the guise of a mining engineer from Ganymede, a Robert Travis. Or possibly as a space-captain's widow, a Mrs. Nordstrom. How did he do it? I'm still not sure. But do it he did."

"I see."

"He's slipped through all our nets—once, twice, a hundred times. But now his luck's running out." Aneido's thick lips drew back. His eyes glinted. "That's why I asked you to come here, tonight, Doctor." He hunched forward still

farther, thumped the arm of the foamex chair. "Together,
you and I, we're going to trap him."

Maurine's feet moved back a fraction closer to her chair.
She sat a little straighter. "But how—"

Aneido laughed. "That comes later, my dear." He bent
over the black case. "It's time we turned this on."

He flipped the switch. My perceptoscope's audio unit
erupted a jumble of squawking sounds. A snowstorm of lines
and blurs swept across the screen, blotting out Maurine,
Aneido, the other room. I swore and worked at the focusing
dials. But it was no use. Aneido's black box was a scrambler
to end all scramblers. After a while I turned the perceptoscope off.

CHAPTER V

THERE was a fabric store just across the street from the
Quiverna. I bought two yards of close-woven, opaque harrah
cloth, took it into the nearest alley and scuffed it in the dirt
till it lost all resemblance to new material. Then, folding it
up again, I tucked it under my—John Raines'—coat and rode
an autotran across the city to where Maurine Dorsett-Burton
lived.

As the voco directory had told me, the building lay on
the fringe of the oldest part of the base development area.
Here there was stone as well as doloid—a shabbiness that
marked this off from the newer units. A thil-shop stood on

the corner, and a drunken crewman from one of the cargo
tramps running the triangle trade routes staggered past as I
got out of the autotran.

I stepped into the building's murky lobby. No one was
there; the place even lacked a desk.

The buzzer board showed a "DR. M. BURTON" in apartment 4-D.

Unfolding my strip of grimy harrah cloth, I draped it over
my arm and waited while the minutes dragged by. Down
the street, a bare-headed, white-haired man hobbled into the
thil-shop. His back had the unmistakable twist that comes
with Mercurian xaython fever. Two heavy-bodied women
with their hair cropped short on the left side after the man-
ner of Europan colonists clumped past me.

I kept on waiting.

Then, somewhere near, an autotran droned. I stepped
back as it rounded the corner and pulled to a smooth halt in
front of the building. Purse in hand, Maurine got out.

I took to the cover of the wall angle at the foot of the
stairs. The door creaked. Footsteps drummed a brisk ca-
dence. I raised the harrah cloth. Maurine rounded the corner. I whipped the cloth down over her face, around her
head.

She kicked, twisted, flailed at me. Tangling her in the
rest of the cloth, I snatched her purse from her hand and
ran out the door, then ducked quickly into the lobby of the
next building.

The purse held the usual hodge-podge; nothing more.
Pocketing the money and tab-lock cards, I shuffled the as-
sorted ID cards, then thumbed through an address book
tucked into a side compartment. The only Fred listed was
surnamed Caudel. He had an address not too far away.

I dropped the purse into the lobby salvage slot and started walking, not pausing till I reached a point across the street from Fred Caudel's apartment building. The place looked cleaner and better kept than Maurine's. Before I could go in, the door opened. A man came out—the same tall, too handsome man I'd met—unpleasantly—at Maurine's office. The man she'd called Fred.

He strode off briskly down the street. I waited till he had a hundred-yard lead, then followed. Two blocks farther on, he turned right, plunging into the cramped streets of the old base area, close to the first port. The thil-shops crowded close against each other, almost one to the drunk, and the air grew heavy with strange smells. Somewhere some sort of drum was booming.

It was a neighborhood where it would be easy to lose a man. I narrowed the gap between us. The drum boomed louder. I could see it now—a percussor mounted on a high street stand beside a doorway just ahead.

The tall man veered as he neared it. Stepping round the stand, he strode into the building. There was a garish sign over the doorway. In glaring scarlet serpentine letters it proclaimed *Chamber of Horrors,* and below that, *Monsters of the Void—Strange Life-Forms from Other Worlds.*

I crossed to it. People were moving around inside. I glimpsed Fred Caudel climbing a narrow stairway at the far end. A woman stood by the door. She had red hair and a mouth to match, and her short spangled jacket was too small across the chest.

"Come on in, mister," she wheedled. "It's only half a credit. We've got things here you won't see anywhere else on Luna—or Terra, either. Transmi from Venus, a Martial dotol, life-forms from every world and satellite. Like this thing. . . ."

She gestured to the street stand. I looked up. An Ionian quontab was chained to the railing. It swayed from side to side, beating the percussor with its shoulder-hammers.

"Only half a credit . . ." the woman repeated loudly.

A sailor from the FedGov fleet pushed past me with his girl.

The redhead leaned back against the door frame, twisting so that the too-tight jacket brushed my arm. "Come on, honey. The lecture starts in just a minute, and afterwards maybe . . ."

She left it hanging. I fumbled a half-credit into her hand and went on in.

Smells hit me in the face: rank smells, fetid smells, smells that were indescribably rotten. I wandered among cases and cages where eye-stalks waved and mandibles bumped plasti-con as they reached for me. Pseudopodal horrors from the cave-swamps of Mercury's Twilight Zone oozed in and out of crevices. Voices went shrill, and men jumped back. There was even a monstrous, ten-tentacled poison zanat, swimming in a sealed tank of refrigerated ammonia and methane.

I worked my way back toward the stairs I'd seen Fred Caudel climbing. A knot of curiosity-seekers had gathered outside, now. The woman's back was toward me. I went up the stairs, three steps at a time.

The door at the top stood half open. I slipped through, into a tiny cubicle of office. No one was in it, but it had a second door. Drawing out my pulsator, I tried the knob. The door was unlocked, and I eased it open the barest crack. I listened, but no sound came.

I opened the door further and stepped into a cramped, garishly furnished living room. It, too, was empty. I locked the door behind me.

Somewhere close at hand, a sudden swish of running water gushed and gurgled. I flattened myself against the wall beside the room's other door and waited. The door opened, and the tall man, the man Maurine had called Fred, came out.

I jabbed the pulsator against him and he crumpled. Working fast, I slit the skin behind his ears, inserted the electrodes from my alternate neurotron, adjusted the sensitometer, pushed the activator contact over. In two minutes I was myself in full control of Fred Caudel's body, looking down through his eyes at the fat, limp, bedraggled, unconscious form of John Raines.

Across the room, the knob of the office door twisted. Tucking in my shirt, I went over and opened the door an inch.

The red-headed woman in the too-tight jacket stood on the other side. "Fred! There was a fellow here—"

"This one?" I opened the door wider, so that she could see Raines.

"Yes!" She slipped inside and clung to me. She was breathing hard. "Who is he, Fred? Do you know him?"

"Yes. He's over at Humanics Research—"

"My God! With Security—"

"No."

"Then what did he want? Is he onto us?"

I shook my head. "Hardly."

"Then why—"

"Why does anyone snoop?" I shrugged. "I think he was just fishing. He picked up an idea somewhere, and now he's trying to fill it out."

"I wish I could be as sure of that as you sound." She looked up at me searchingly. Her face might have been almost pretty without the thick, smeared makeup. "How much longer will it be, Fred? Before you get the rest of the dope you need from that Burton bitch, I mean. You said it wouldn't take you but another day or two."

I said, "It won't. Believe me, it won't."

"Tomorrow, maybe?"

"Maybe."

"And then, to sell it to those Mek bastards, those master minds . . ." The woman shivered convulsively against me. "I hope it's worth it, Fred. Because if anything goes wrong—"

"Nothing's going wrong." I broke away from her and knelt beside Raines. "Get me some tape."

"What?"

"For his eyes."

"Oh." She crossed to a cabinet, came back with a roll of adhesive. "Here."

"Thanks." I began sealing strips across his lids in a gummy, impenetrable blindfold.

"A million credits!" The woman rolled the sum over her tongue as if she liked the taste of it, in spite of all her doubts. "Do you think they'll really pay it, Fred? Even the Meks are going to think a long time before they put out that kind of money."

"They'll pay it," I clipped. I strapped Raines' wrists tight together with his belt. "They'll say it's cheap at the price."

"I wish I could be sure. If we can just get away with it . . . go off someplace, a million miles from them damn' geeks downstairs. They stink so, and every time you go past you can see those slimy eye-stalks waving. Sometimes I think I just can't stand it any more. . . ." The woman's voice trailed off. She gestured to Raines. "What happens to him?"

I went to work on his ankles with a strip torn from his shirt. "I'll put him away for a while."

"Not . . . for good?"

"No. Not unless something happens."

"Thank God for that," the woman breathed hoarsely. "I don't think I could take murder."

I finished Raines' ankles and got up. "Forget it."

"I can't forget it." She was pressing against me again, hanging on me. "I'm scared, Fred. I'm so scared I don't know what I'm doing."

I held her for a moment. "There's nothing to be afraid of."

"It's this whole business." She shuddered. "What goes on in her mind, Fred? That Burton slut, I mean. This projecto-scope thing—it's awful! To reach into a man's head, drag out his thoughts . . . Just the idea of it gives me the creeps!"

To reach into a man's head, drag out his thoughts . . .

I stood very still.

"No wonder Security wants it," the woman whispered. "Think what it'll mean, Fred. Screen a Mek with it—he don't even have to talk; they'll still nail him. What chance will sharpies like us stand?"

She was shivering again. I gripped her shoulders. "Easy, Red. You've got to relax."

"I can't. Talk just won't do it. There aren't any words . . ." She writhed. "This damn' jacket! It's too tight. Open it, Fred."

I began, "This is no time—"

Her fingers twisted into my hair. She pulled my face down. The red mouth trembled against mine. "Open it, damn you!"

I was glad I'd tied Raines. . . .

CHAPTER VI

I DROPPED by Maurine Dorsett-Burton's office at Humanics Research early the next work-cycle. I didn't bother to knock.

Maurine stood beside her desk, holding a black-framed picture. She looked up, almost too quickly, as I came in, and laid the picture face down on the desk.

"Fred . . ." Her eyes were a trifle red.

"And good morning to you, too," I said.

She didn't smile. "You know you're not supposed to be here."

I brought out my wallet, riffled through the cards. "This" —I extended the right one—"says Fred Caudel is a technician assigned to Electro-Neural Testing."

"But not to this project." She squared the picture with the edge of her desk. Tiny lines crisscrossed her forehead as her dark brows drew together. "You can't seem to understand that my work is top secret. If Security were to find you here—"

"—we'd both be in trouble. The trouble is, you're in trouble already, only you won't admit it. This kind of trouble."

I leaned across her desk as I spoke, and picked up the picture. It was a portrait of a man, keen-eyed and broad across the forehead, with hair graying at the temples.

Color touched Maurine's cheeks. She lifted the portrait from my hand and put it into a drawer. "There are times when you remind me of John Raines, Fred—and that isn't a compliment."

"I still say you can't live with it."

"A widow has to have something to hold to, Fred."

"Maurine . . ." I fumbled. "I'm sorry."

"There's no need to be. It's just that—"

She broke off, turned, picked up a folder. I couldn't see her face.

I ran my palm along my pant-leg. "How's the project coming?"

She kept her face averted. Her voice held a tiny thread of strain. "Sometimes I wonder about you, Fred. It's as if you were trying to get into trouble, as if you wanted Security to clamp down on you . . ."

I didn't say anything.

She said, "You remind me of another man I knew once, years ago. Alan Lord was his name. He pushed the same way you do. He liked trouble, danger."

I folded my arms, cupping my sweating hands over the biceps, and held my hip hard against the desk. "What happened to him?"

"He . . . became a Mechanist. It was that headstrong streak he had; that, and a strange, warped sort of idealism. I think he really believed that science was everything." A faraway note crept into Maurine's voice. "I tried to show him that people weren't robots, and how the Somex couldn't help but grow into a tyranny worse than the FedGov ever dreamed of being. But he couldn't see it. So . . . he went his way, and I went mine."

"Did you . . . love him?"

The papers rattled in the folder.

I said, "Don't answer that, Maurine. Only a ghoul like me would ask it. Let's talk about your project."

"It's—it's all right."

"Have you heard anything more from Security?"

The folder slapped down on the desk. "You're determined to get into trouble, aren't you?"

I shrugged. "I'll leave if you tell me to."

"No." Straight and slim, eyes level now, she faced me. "Maybe that's what I want, too. To get into trouble."

"With Security?"

"With someone. I guess I don't care who." She turned. "I'm running a test on a new case this morning. You can help me."

I followed her into the laboratory room behind the office. Bare, blue-white walls gave it an aseptic look. The furnishings were limited to a table and two chairs. A bulky apparatus equipped with what looked like a reader screen stood on the table.

Maurine pressed a buzzer. Almost at once, a side door opened. An attendant led in a shambling, blank-faced man. He had the loose mouth and unfocused eyes of someone who had wandered into a Somex laboratory's mind-shield.

Maurine rested her hand on the back of the chair directly in front of the screen. "Put him here, please." And then, when the attendant had seated the blank-faced man in the chair: "You can go now. I'll buzz you when I'm through."

The attendant left.

Maurine handed me a jar. "Here. Grease his temples."

I obeyed.

Lifting a strange, helmet-like metal casing out from behind the screen, Maurine began adjusting set-screws. "Now grease that ridge behind his ears. And stripe the center of his forehead from the hairline down to the bridge of his nose."

I smeared on more of the goo in the jar.

Head tilted, Maurine inspected the job. "Good. He's ready for the cap."

I picked up the metal casing. Electrodes projected inside it at points corresponding to the spots I'd smeared. Setting it down on the shorty's head, I adjusted the contacts, then clamped the chin-piece tight.

"Don't forget to strap his arms and legs, too. Sometimes the first impulse startles them, you know."

I looked behind the screen, found another helmet and a tangle of straps. In less than a minute I had the shorty anchored as directed.

Maurine held the jar now. She was greasing her own head in the same pattern as the patient's. That done, she put on the second helmet, then handed me two cables, each connected to the apparatus behind the screen.

"You can plug us in now."

The plugs were eight-contact females. Eight metal prongs thrust up from the crown of each helmet. I plugged the cables to them. Maurine stepped back to the control panel of the apparatus behind the screen and threw a switch, then worked intently over an assortment of dials and indicators. A faint humming sound rose.

She straightened. "All right, now. We'll give him a quick run, first. Just don't say anything."

She clicked a knob to the right.

The blank-faced man stiffened against the straps. His mouth twitched.

Maurine stepped around beside me, in front of the screen, and raised a stiff white card. "Dog."

Nothing happened.

"Mother."

There was a faint flickering on the screen—an ebb and flow of shadowy patterns.

"Hate."

The patterns faded.

"Somex."

Nothing at all.

"Wife."

Shadow-patterns, perhaps a trifle stronger than those in response to the word *mother*.

"Ink."

A blank screen.

"Knife."

Nothing.

"Kiss."

A momentary flutter.

Maurine walked back to the control board, clicked the knob left. "You see?" The cool beauty of her face was shadowed. She smoothed the coil of dark hair in the old, familiar gesture. "On most words, there's no response at all. Even the ones that touch the deepest roots, the closest interpersonal relationships, only bring shadows."

I nodded slowly.

"There's a synaptic inhibition, Fred. A block's been set up against memory, against association. That's the only explanation. Here"—she thrust the white card at me—"try me. See the difference."

I took the card. She turned another notch left this time.

I read the first word on the card: "Dog."

The screen flickered. A brown mongrel bounded across it, leaping and frisking.

"Mother."

A white-haired woman appeared. Then, in a flash, the scene changed. The same woman, younger this time, stood laughing by a table, holding a candle-sparkling birthday cake. The next instant she lay in bed—old again, eyes and cheeks sunken.

"Hate."

The screen blurred. Here and there, unrelated fragments flashed through; that was all.

Maurine said, "You see? Hate's an abstraction. You can't get too clear a picture from it without more specific stimulus, except in paranoid cases."

I nodded, read the next word: "Somex."

My own face stared up at me from the screen. Not Fred Caudel's face, but my own—the face of Alan Lord as he had looked those twelve long years ago.

The knob on the control board clicked. The screen went blank.

Maurine said, "That's enough of that. We'd better get back to our case study." Her face was pale, her eyes on the dials of the apparatus.

I nodded, not speaking.

"We'll run him through the entire list this time, then try to rebuild associational relationships in the areas where we get the best responses." She was Doctor Burton to the hilt, now—all cool poise and brisk efficiency. "I've never told you, Fred, but I've got a theory about these cases. And it won't be mere theory much longer if these tests develop the way I think they will."

I pretended to check the electrodes on the blank-faced shorty's helmet. "A theory? What is it?"

For a moment her fingertips drummed the table. Her face grew serious. "I imagine you know that the brain comes close to being a sort of electro-chemical computer?"

"Yes."

"To break it down even further, each neuron is a tiny dynamo, producing current. The neurons connect by inter-meshing synapses, by contact only. The synapses act as switches, routing the nerve current from one neuron to an-other."

"That's basic neurology."

"The synapses can act as circuit-breakers, too."

I straightened. "What?"

"They're organic electrical equipment. They can be over-loaded."

"In which case—"

"They break the circuit. Or even short-circuit." Maurine's eyes were suddenly alight with, excitement. She leaned on the projectoscope. "Don't you see? It happens in neurosis and psychosis every day, Fred. First, inhibition blocks the free flow of nerve current. An overload piles up. Finally the synapses can't handle it any longer—and you have break-down."

"But what's that got to do with him?" I gestured to the shorty.

Maurine's lips curved in a slow smile. Her voice dropped a note. "What if it were possible to project an overload into a man's brain, Fred—a sudden, overpowering electrical pulsa-tion keyed to the same frequency as human nerve current? Mightn't it precipitate a complete, permanent, synaptic block—an artificial amnesia? Because that's what's wrong with this poor thing! He's suffering from chronic synaptic inhibition. His brain synapses won't pass on thought impulses from neuron to neuron—so his whole associate processes have broken down."

I sat down on the edge of the table. "It's a good theory, Maurine. But I don't see how it could happen."

"I do," she retorted. "I can see Somex centers hidden on every satellite and planet—with a shielding system around each one to shoot an electrical overload into any brain that came too close."

My lips were suddenly stiff. I said, "That's nonsense. You haven't any proof—"

"Not yet." She stood erect once more, her lovely face mask-like. "Give me the word-card, please. We'll run another test. You may chart the record; the forms are over here."

"And by whose permission may he chart the record?" a deep voice demanded.

I whirled.

In the office doorway stood General Aneido, stiff-necked and grim. Two cold-faced Security operatives in mufti waited close behind him.

"I asked a question, Doctor." He bit off his words. "What is this man doing here?"

Maurine stood cool and straight. Her cheeks were a trifle pale. "I asked him to assist me."

"Without regard for security regulations? In spite of the fact that I warned you less than a cycle ago that your work must be kept a complete secret?"

Maurine's expression did not change. "He was cleared by your own staff before being assigned to duty at Humanics Research—"

"But he wasn't cleared for work on this project!" The general strode on into the room—his face flushed, jaw jutting. "I'm not accustomed to having my orders disregarded so blithely, Doctor."

I broke in: "It's my fault, General. I was interested—"

"And how did you learn about the project? Where did you find out enough to become interested?"

"I—"

"Quiet, Fred." Maurine rested her hand on the projectoscope. "General Aneido, has it occurred to you that this device is my own development? That I've spent years on it, discussed it a hundred times with my colleagues here in Electro-Neural Testing before you ever heard of it? Security or no security, I needed their help as fellow-scientists—"

Abruptly, Aneido brought up a broad, blunt hand. "That's enough, Doctor Burton. We'll take up the security violation later, through the proper channels. What I want now is evidence that this apparatus"—he gestured to the projectoscope —"will do the things you say it will."

"Of course." Maurine adjusted the metal casing on her head. "The theory's fairly simple. It's based on the fact that all mental activity is really a conditioned channeling of electrical discharges into subjective perceptual images in response to specific stimuli."

"Can you put that in layman's language, Doctor?"

"I can oversimplify it, perhaps, by saying that whether you're conscious of it or not, thoughts flash pictures in your brain."

"I see."

"My projectoscope simply transfers those pictures onto a screen." Maurine touched each element as she spoke. "I use this Talodak unit, here, to boost the nerve current to the point where it will activate an inversion of the old Renkinov stimulator, linked to an extremely sensitive artificial retina—"

Again, Aneido brought up his hand. "The technical details mean nothing to me, Doctor Burton. As I told you last night, the practical applications are all I'm interested in. If this device will show men's thoughts so that I can uncover secret Meks, that's all I ask. I want to see a test."

"Certainly." Maurine stepped back and turned to the two Security agents. "If one of you gentlemen will just sit down—"

"No!" clipped Aneido.

"Then what—"

The general leveled a blunt forefinger at me. "We'll test this man here. You claim he's safe. Now we'll find out!"

I shrugged, slipped my hand into my pocket. "Anything you say, General." My fingers brushed the pulsator.

"Of course." Maurine motioned me to the empty chair. "Sit down, Fred."

I obeyed. With quick efficiency, she greased my head, then transferred the shorty's helmet to me. "I use a word-association system for primary stimulus, General Aneido. Each word, read aloud to the subject, sets off a reaction pattern. The mental pictures that result are projected through the artificial retina onto the screen. After that, it's just a matter of interpretation."

"I see," Aneido nodded grimly. He held out his hand. "Give me your word list."

"What—"

"I'll read it myself, in whatever order I choose." The general's lips drew back in the same wolf-grin I'd seen the night before. "You see, I don't trust you, Doctor. Not after finding this man here. I'm taking no chances on collusion."

"I—I see." Tiny lines of strain etched Maurine's face.

"The card, please, Doctor."

"Yes. Yes, of course." She handed it to him. I thought I could see her fingers trembling.

I gripped the pulsator.

"I'm ready, Doctor." There was an ugly glint in Aneido's eyes.

"Very well." Maurine's eyes were on the projectoscope's control panel.

She clicked the knob. It was as if someone had struck a gong in the top of my head—more startling than painful. My temples pulsed and throbbed.

"Mother," clipped Aneido.

A white-haired woman's face flashed on the screen—the same face that had come when I read the word *mother* to Maurine.

For an instant I stared, while more associational images centering on the woman flashed past. Then, shifting, I stole a glance past the screen to the control board.

Maurine hadn't moved. Her hand still rested on the knob. But it was turned left, not right.

CHAPTER VII

I LOOKED out of the window of Fred Caudel's apartment, down into the street. There was the usual traffic. Over to the right, a Security man lounged in a doorway and cleaned his fingernails.

I swung round and peered left. Another loiterer with "Security" written all over him leaned against a thil-shop window and scanned the news-reader inside. Fred Caudel's time was running out.

I took a light-bath and changed clothes, then went into the kitchen and scrambled together a quick lunch of sliced canna and gesk-meat sandwiches, washed down with a tube of foamy purple Venusian yar-beer. By the time I'd finished, a third Security man was standing talking to the first.

Leaving the apartment, I went downstairs and peeked out the building's rear entrance. Security had it covered, too.

I went on down another flight of stairs to the base level and hunted up the climatizer room.

A young husky looked up as I came in. He had a big brindle cat on his lap. The spray of blue pockmarks along one side of his face said he wouldn't make any more space trips; probably that was why he was here now, looking after a second-rate apartment building for a living.

He said, "Hi, Mr. Caudel."

"Hi," I grinned back. "Look, a friend of mine with Security asked me to check up on something. Where's the trap door down here?"

"The trap door?" The husky looked blank.

"Yes. All these old buildings have shafts that go down to refuge tunnels. They dug 'em back during the Chaos, when they were afraid the atomic wars on Earth might spread to Luna."

"Oh." The caretaker scratched the back of the cat's head absently. "Yeah, I guess I know what you mean."

He got up, sliding the cat to the floor, and led me back to the stairway. "Here. Is this what you're talking about?"

It was a manhole, set in the floor behind the stairs.

I scraped the rim clean with my foot. "Let's see if we can get the cover off."

"Sure. There's a ring, see?" He bent, heaved. The lid came free.

I looked down into the black shaft. There was a metal ladder set into the wall. "That's it, all right."

"That's all you wanted?"

"That's all," I nodded. "Come on up to my place and have a drink. You can put the lid back later."

"Gee, thanks, Mr. Caudel."

He followed me up the stairs. I brought out my pulsator under cover of my tab-card. When he stepped through the doorway ahead of me, I touched him with it.

Five minutes later I was back at the manhole, a young husky with a blue-pocked face. Fred Caudel lay snoring on his own bed upstairs.

I lowered myself into the shaft and slid the manhole cover shut above me, then descended the metal ladder. It went down a long way—fifty feet or more, as nearly as I could figure. At the bottom I felt my way around the shaft wall till I found the thick, lead-sheathed door.

It had a lever handle instead of a lock. I opened it and stepped out into the cold, greenish glow of a radiation lamp set in a wall bracket. The distant gleam of other lamps marked a broad passageway that stretched off both to right and left—the last, half-forgotten relic of a terror long dead.

I trotted left through the tunnel's sifting dust till my legs began to tire, then got out my com-set and sat down against the wall beneath one of the coldly glowing lamps.

This time the duty man gave me Zero without question.

"Yes, Four-four?"

I said, "The trouble's started, Zero. The real trouble."

"What do you mean, Four-four?" The words were calm, but his voice had a raw edge.

"You remember that I told you a woman might be the key

to this whole business—all Project X, both segments A and B?"

"Yes."

"She's developed an outfit that picks your thoughts right out of your mind. It reacts as spontaneously as your brain does. So far as I can see, there's no way to beat it."

"Does Security know about it?"

"Aneido himself. That's why he came to Luna. He'd have caught me for sure if the woman hadn't tricked him."

"She . . . tricked him?"

"Yes."

"Why?"

"I don't know."

There was a moment of silence. Then Zero asked, "Is it possible she's a sympathizer, Four-four?"

"No. Definitely not."

"Perhaps she knows more about the personality you're currently wearing than you do, and was afraid for him—what he might reveal about himself."

"It could be."

More silence.

I said, "There's more, Zero. She's figured out what's happened to the shorties. All of it."

I could hear him suck in breath. "Then Four-four, you're on the ground. What do you recommend?"

I grunted. "I'm afraid it's not my day for recommending. For once, I can't see any angle."

"Four-four . . ."

I waited.

"Could you route this woman to The Center? By the end of the next cycle?"

I twisted sharply. "What—"

Zero's voice was grim, savage. "I know it's going to rush you. But this crisis—there's only one answer. We've got to revise our whole timetable, push it ahead. Getting the woman's a major step."

I was breathing too fast. "What good would that do? There's bound to be plans for her gadget on file in a dozen places. We can't get them all. And Aneido—"

"Aneido may prove to be the least of our worries," Zero cut in on me harshly. And then, after a pause: "The tests on Process Q are completed. It's ready for use."

"Process Q?" I frowned and ran my thumb along the com-set. "That's new to me. What is it?"

Zero chuckled. His voice had lost some of its tension. "It's our road to power, Four-four. Our top 'top secret.' "

"But what—"

"It will . . . replace . . . the general."

I gripped the com-set. "Zero! Is this a joke?"

"Hardly." He clipped the word. "We haven't any choice, Four-four. Not after what you've told me. So . . . General Aneido will be treated by Process Q. He becomes our first non-experimental subject."

I groped for words. "But how—"

"You know where he's located, don't you?"

"Of course. We've got a plant in the next apartment."

"Good. The equipment can be set up there. We'll rush Nine-seven in from our Luna lab to take care of the technical side of it. You can pick him up at the secret station."

I leaned back against the wall. Talking suddenly seemed like a waste of time.

"Route the general to The Center, also," Zero continued.

"That's why I want the woman here. She can demonstrate her apparatus on him. We'll need all the information we can drain out of him to put this thing over. And Four-four . . ."

"Yes."

A little of the grimness left Zero's voice. "This woman— was I right, before? Was she the one you . . . used to know?"

I shifted. "Does it matter?"

"I think it does." He was Zero, my friend, now; not the chill, impersonal Zero who directed the far-flung affairs of the Society of Mechanists on every satellite and planet. "We need her, Four-four. We need her badly. But you still love her, and she's not one of us, so you'll be . . . tempted."

I stared down at the com-set's grillwork. "You know me awfully well, don't you, Zero?"

"Yes, I know you." He said it almost sadly. "I know you because I know myself, Four-four. It's that reckless, head-strong streak of yours that brought us together. I've got it, too."

"I hadn't noticed."

"Just don't let it get out of hand, Four-four. Not now when we're so close to victory. The work you've done—the Society won't forget it. And once your sweetheart's here, you can be together."

I scuffed the dust of the passageway with my toe.

Zero said, "It's settled, then, Four-four. Process Q for Aneido; then route both him and the woman to The Center. Right?" His tone was brisk again, incisive.

I stared off through the darkness, down the long line of cold, green, glowing radiation lamps that marked the passage. The utter stillness pressed in on me.

The com-set buzzed. "Right, Four-four?" Zero prodded.

"Right," I answered dully.

I kept on staring at the radiation lamps for a long, long time.

CHAPTER VIII

ANOTHER cog-train thundered into the transit center. Brakes screamed and couplings rattled. Then the bars went down. Miners poured out of the pneumocars, yelling and laughing: thick-shouldered, heavy-chested men, in for a cycle or two or three here at the great port base. Around the cycle, they came and they went—cog-trains and miners, up from the Mare Nubium fields and the Leibnitz Mountains; outbound for the pits at Schickard and the giant shaft south of Lacus Somniorum.

I leaned back in my seat and relaxed and watched Street Exit D. No one gave me a second glance. Blue pockmarks and stained brotex work clothes were too common.

A new crowd surged in from the street: more miners, outbound; girls from the thil-shops, down to see them off; a stray spaceman or two.

One of the girls stepped out of the rush and paused. She was a tall girl, with tawny hair. I got up and wandered over closer to her. It was Narla Cherritt.

She was frowning and scanning the crowd. I drifted around beside her, as if I were looking for someone, too. She glanced at me, then turned away.

I said, "Zero," holding my voice low.

Her hands tightened convulsively on her purse. That was all. She didn't even look around at me again.

"Who are you looking for?"

"A—a fat man. He's short, with watery eyes—"

"John Raines?"

"Yes." Her lips trembled. "Where is he? I've got to find him."

"Why?"

"He—he was to meet my contact here."

"And your contact sent you instead?" I swore under my breath.

"No, no; my contact doesn't even know I'm here."

"What—"

"I'm telling the truth! Really I am! Raines . . . tried to help me once. And now—"

She broke off, lips stiff and quivering. Her knuckles were white against the purse.

"Raines hasn't come yet," I clipped. "If something's wrong, tell me. This may be the only chance you'll get."

Her head came round. She looked at me—a long, searching look. She was so pale I was afraid she was going to faint.

She whispered, "My contact—he's turned Raines in to Security. They'll be here any minute."

"And you're a Bek." I said it bitterly. "Even if Heffner turns yellow, you'll carry on and save the day for the Society."

"No! That isn't it at all!" Tears brimmed her eyes. She bent her head quickly. "I'm not a Mechanist—not now. I'm doing this just for Mr. Raines . . . because he tried to help me. When Heffner finds out, he'll turn me in, too."

I didn't say anything. I couldn't.

"That funny little fat man! He said you couldn't be human and be a Mechanist, too."

"He was right."

"Yes. I know that now. I've thought it through."

I said, "I'll tell Raines that—"

The girl caught her breath. I pivoted, following her eyes. Uniformed Security men were filing through Street Exit D into the station.

I said, "Take it easy. They're looking for a fat man named Raines. They don't know us."

Security men were pouring in through the other entrances now, forming a cordon. The station speaker boomed: "Attention! Stand by to have your papers checked! No one may leave the station until his papers have been examined!"

I slapped at the pockets of my current personality's stained brotex work clothes. There was a handkerchief, a tool-knife, a writer, a wad of crumpled credit notes and a few coins. No identity papers.

The Security men began herding the station crowd into groups. A corporal and two privates bore down on the girl and me.

I moved in between them and Narla Cherritt. Out of the corner of my mouth I clipped, "Quick! Was Heffner your only contact? Did anyone else know you were a Mek?"

Her lips were white. "No. Just Heffner—"

"Then leave everything to me. Don't admit anything!"

The Security men closed in. The corporal snapped, "You two! Let's see your ID's!"

Narla fumbled in her purse.

I fell back a step. "What'sa matter? Can't a mono pick up a girl in a thil-shop any more without you lead-heads buttin' in?"

The corporal grabbed my hand and jerked it up, palm out. "Don't try to guff me! Not with a mitt soft as that! You're no mono!"

"And this wench never come out of no thil-shop, neither!" a private echoed.

The other private was circling. He grabbed my arms from behind, twisted them up in a break-lock. "Here! I got 'im!"

The corporal ran his hands over me. "So! No papers, huh?" He jerked a thumb over his shoulder. "Take him along!"

"What about the wench?" It was the other private talking. "Her card looks all right."

"She's with him, ain't she? She goes, too."

"Hey, wait a minute!" I tried to twist free of the break-lock.

The corporal slammed me in the chest with the heel of his hand; he hit me so hard I would have fallen if the private hadn't been holding me. "On your way!"

They shoved us toward the exit, through the cordon and out of the station.

Big vansters were waiting, a whole row of them. They had tailgate doors of heavy grating. Our captors hurried us down the line to the last one, parked close to the high fence of the cog-train yard. A dozen sullen-faced prisoners were already aboard. They were shifty-eyed specimens—petty criminals, mostly, or ship-jumpers from the cargo fleet.

The private let go of my arms. "Up, you!" The corporal was already lifting Narla aboard.

I swung my hands around, windmill fashion.

"Go on! Get up!"

"You ever tried to climb with your arms twisted half off?" I snarled back. I reached into my pocket, palmed a wadded credit note, brought out my handkerchief and swabbed my neck.

"Listen, you—"

"I'm going. I'm going." I stuffed the handkerchief back into my pocket, reached up and grasped the door frame at lock level, and swung up, cramming the wadded bill into the bolt-slot with my thumb.

An officer clipped, "That's enough for this load. You men can ride guard." He turned to our group, the prisoners. "There'll be a man with a paragun on the roof. His orders are to shoot to kill if you start anything."

I stole a glance back at the bolt-slot. The wadded bill didn't show.

The tailgate grating clanged shut. The private who'd checked Narla's papers jumped on outside.

I crowded next to her. "Did he keep your card?"

"No."

"Then get ready."

The vanster jerked, lumbered forward. Turning right around the end of the fence, it jounced over the tracks. I craned to one side. Ahead, a cog-train engine puffed and snorted, just short of our right-of-way.

I slipped out the tool-knife and flicked open the thin blade. Leaning against the door grating, I held the private's eyes with mine. "What'sa matter, anyhow? What brought all this on?" I slid the knife blade between door and frame as I spoke, wedging the point into the bolt-slot, prying and twisting.

The private turned to spit. "Trouble. Mek trouble."

"But we ain't Meks." I pried harder.

"Tell that to Headquarters."

The bolt clicked back, and I started breathing again.

The noise of the cog-train engine had risen over the rattling and jouncing of the vanster. We were abreast it now. It towered over us.

"Narla . . ."

"Yes."

I kicked the tailgate door heard. It slammed back, carrying the private outside with it.

I was jumping before he hit the ground. When he tried to rise, I kicked him in the face. Narla Cherritt jumped after me, tripped and fell. I caught her up bodily and ran for the engine. Over my shoulder, I glimpsed the man on top of the vanster swinging round his paragun.

Before he could fire, the cog-train was between us. I raced back along the engine to the cab's ladder and clawed my way up.

The engineer turned in his seat as I topped the floor sill. I shoved the tool knife at him and snarled, "Get it rolling! Fast!"

He jerked levers. The cog-train jolted forward, picking up speed.

I let the girl down and looked back. The vanster was a mess. Prisoners were running every which way, and the Security men didn't seem to know quite what to do about it.

We dropped off the engine at the next crossway and left the yards. After that there was an autotran, more walking, another autotran, and finally the Quiverna.

Narla Cherritt's face was still drawn and pale. She looked up at the building as if it were paradise molded in vitraline and chromoid. Her words came out stumbling and ragged: "I—I don't know what to say . . ."

"Then don't say it." I pushed open the autotran's door. "It's time I got busy on something else."

"Of course." She got out quickly.

I said, "One detail: Don't worry about Heffner. He won't bother you again." Then I shoved the autotran's tracer ahead fast in an aimless pattern. Maybe there were tears on her cheeks. Or it could have been the way the light fell as the autotran pulled away.

I stopped off at the nearest voco station and dialed Heffner's number. He answered in seconds.

I said, "Mr. Heffner, this is Security, Base Headquarters unit. We've got that man Raines. We want you to come down and identify him right away."

He could hardly wait to hang up. I brought the autotran back around to the Quiverna port and left it, taking my own stand by the fabric shop where I'd bought the harrah cloth earlier.

Heffner came out of the Quiverna's entrance in less than two minutes. He headed straight for the autotran I'd just left. I waited till he was almost there, rolling my pulsator back and forth between my thumb and fingers. He didn't even waste a glance on me.

When he reached for the door handle, I stepped forward. I was in the way when he turned to close the door behind him. He stared at me blankly. "What—"

Crowding into the autotran, I said, "This is a little present from Narla Cherritt."

I waited till I saw the fear leap in his eyes before I touched him.

CHAPTER IX

NINE-SEVEN said, "Yes, Mr. Heffner, we're ready."

I looked at my new face in the wall mirror: Heffner's face. There were the beady little black eyes, the pinched features, the sallow parchment skin, the balding head. Mine, now. For a while.

Nine-seven cleared his throat. "Mr. Heffner—"

"Yes, I heard you." I gave myself a wry grin and turned to the maze of equipment set up in Heffner's bedroom. We'd pushed the furniture back against the walls to make room for a tank some seven feet long and a row of smaller tanks that connected with it. Beside that stood a metal case with a hinged lid; it looked something like a twentieth century burial casket. The wall that adjoined Aneido's living room was lined with a whole row of devices whose names I didn't even know, and there was enough cable coiling here and there to rewire the building.

I said, "Look, I know the technical end of this thing is none of my business, but I'd at least like to get the outline."

The corners of Nine-seven's mouth pulled up, as if he had to plan to be amused. "Certainly, Mr. Heffner. I'll explain as we go along." He bent to straighten out a cable. He did it with a neat precision that said order meant a lot to him. So did his appearance, for that matter—every hair in place, clothes that might as well have been a uniform, the bleak lack of color in his face and voice.

There were a lot like him in the Society.

He straightened again. "The first step is the hypnojector. Have you ever used it?"

"No."

"It amounts to an inversion of the perceptoscope. You won't have any trouble understanding it."

He stepped over and got the perceptoscope going. Slowly, the screen cleared and the image sharpened.

General Aneido sat in the same foamex chair he'd occupied when I looked in on him and Maurine. As before, he was clicking microbook frames through the reader.

Nine-seven moved over to the next machine. "Be quiet now, please. This device has both audio and video elements."

He turned a dial. A faint, pulsing, monotonous drone arose from the machine, and he shot an anxious glance at the perceptoscope's scanner screen, then whispered, "We have to bleed the drone in carefully. If it came up too fast, it might catch the subject's attention."

I nodded. On the screen, Aneido continued his reading undisturbed.

Nine-seven turned another dial. A small screen at the top of the hypnojector lighted up.

At first I couldn't see any image on it. Then I blinked. There was movement *without* image—a sort of seething, as if sand were simmering slowly in water.

Nine-seven pointed to the perceptoscope. Aneido was blinking, too. He rubbed his eyes.

Nine-seven turned the audio dial up a notch. The drone grew louder. The seconds ticked by, and Aneido blinked some more and shook his head. Then his lids lowered and stayed closed. Slowly, his heavy chin sank onto his chest.

Nine-seven turned up the dial another notch and whis-

pered, "Now . . . the vocal channel!" He moved a lever,
picked up what looked like a voco mouth unit, and spoke
into it in a low, gently coaxing voice: "Sleep, Aneido . . .
sleep . . . sleep . . . a deep sleep . . . a sleep so deep you
cannot waken . . ."

I was looking at the perceptoscope's scanner screen. General Aneido was shifting uneasily. He slumped lower in his
chair.

Nine-seven kept on talking: "You cannot waken, Aneido.
You cannot. You've never slept so deep a sleep before. Now
you can't even lift your hand. Try, Aneido. Try to lift your
hand. . . ."

The general's right hand twitched. His body twisted. But
the hand didn't rise.

"Such a deep sleep . . ." Nine-seven whispered. "So deep,
so deep. Your muscles are like water. . . ."

Aneido's head sagged to one side. His heavy body had a
sodden look.

"Try to lift your hand again, Aneido. Try hard! You can
lift it now. . . ."

Even in the screen, I could see the beads of sweat start on
Aneido's face. His body heaved. Slowly, shakily, the right
hand came up.

"Try to get up, Aneido. Stand up! Stand up!"

Aneido gripped the arms of the foamex chair. The muscles
along his jaw stood out. Like a statue coming to life, he rose
from the chair and stood swaying.

"Open your eyes, Aneido. . . ."

The lined lids lifted. The eyes stared, blank and glassy.

"Aneido! Listen carefully! The Somex has another plot
afoot, but you can smash it! There's a man in the next apartment who knows about it. He'll help you. Go to him. Listen

to him. Obey him! Go to the next apartment now, Aneido—apartment seven-three-three! You can smash the Mechanists if you do! You'll have power—more power than you ever dreamed of! Go! Go to seven-three-three! The door is open. . . ."

Aneido was already moving. Shuffling, eyes glazed, head sunk down between his heavy shoulders, he lumbered across the frame toward his own apartment's door.

Nine-seven pivoted. "Quick! Open the door!"

I ran into the living room and jerked the door open, stepping aside and behind it.

The veldrene carpet whispered. Through the crack along the hinges, I saw General Aneido appear in the hall. Like an automaton, he turned when he reached our door and shuffled past me into the room.

"This way, Aneido," Nine-seven said softly. He backed toward the bedroom doorway. "This way. In here."

Dog-like, Aneido followed him.

Nine-seven reached the side of the metal casket. He lifted the lid. "Here, Aneido. Lie here. . . ."

Aneido reached the threshold of the bedroom and stood swaying. His head rolled from side to side.

"Aneido!" Nine-seven said sharply. "This way, Aneido—"

Abruptly, Aneido stopped swaying. His head came up from between his shoulders. His right hand lifted in a quick arc. "Another time, Mek."

He said it almost gently, but it was the same deep voice I'd heard before. It had iron in it. I didn't need to see his face or the gun I knew he held in his hand. That voice, and Nine-seven's gray lips, were enough.

"Mek ego!" Aneido chuckled mirthlessly. "There's nothing like it. . . ."

Nine-seven's Adam's apple moved up and down. His eyes had a white panic-rim around the iris.

I slid my pulsator out of my pocket and stepped from behind the door, barely breathing.

"Security found out about your hypnotic gadget over a year ago," the general observed conversationally. "Our psych staff drummed the whole drone-and-blur business into our heads till we could recognize them in our sleep."

Nine-seven's eyes flicked this way and that. In a tremulous voice he said, "I'm afraid I'm going to be sick," and leaned against the metal casket.

I took a slow, silent step forward. Then another.

Aneido was studying Nine-seven now. "You're Gervault, aren't you? Doctor Hercule Cervault, the top biochemist of the Venusian colonies, till you disappeared." He shook his massive head. "Why did you do it, Gervault? What is there about your lunatic Society of Mechanists that makes men like you throw away your lives?"

Nine-seven's face was a sweat-splotched mask. "For God's sake—"

"And what has God got to do with it? You Mechanists don't believe in God."

I took another step.

"You're frightened, Gervault. That's all that's wrong. But you don't need to be. . . ." Aneido's voice dropped a note. "You'd be more use to me alive and free than in a cell—if you'd just talk."

I took still another step. I was close now—almost close enough.

Aneido said, "Your friend behind me could save his neck, too, Gervault. A place on the budget council's better than a grave."

My belly muscles convulsed. I lunged by pure reflex.

Only Aneido was already side-stepping and whirling. It was a pretty piece of footwork, faster than his bulk gave me any reason to expect. The muzzle of his paragun whipped round. And I was still clawing for balance.

Nine-seven slammed the casket lid. For the fraction of a second Aneido's smooth flow of motion broke. I rammed the pulsator against him. He went down like a falling zanat.

I leaned against the bedroom door jamb, panting. I could hardly hold onto the pulsator. Nine-seven ran for the bathroom. He'd meant it when he said he was going to be sick.

When he came out, his hair was slicked smooth again, and his mouth had the old precise set. He looked down at Aneido as if the general were a biological specimen on the dissecting board. "You shouldn't have done that, Four-four."

"I shouldn't have done what?"

"Used your pulsator. I don't know what effect it will have on Process Q."

I just stared at him.

He said, "We'd better get to work. Close the outside door."

I obeyed. When I came back, he was busy stripping Aneido.

"Now help me lift him into the matrix chamber."

Together, we carried the naked general over and heaved him into the metal casket. Nine-seven adjusted clamps to hold him, then closed the lid and began twisting dials. "Do you know what a pantograph is?" His voice was dry, professorial.

"You mean one of those affairs they use sometimes to scale maps and pictures?"

"Correct. All this"—Nine-seven indicated the sprawling mass of equipment—"constitutes a sort of electro-biochemical pantograph. It duplicates and conditions cell structures."

"What—"

"All living matter is made up of cells and their products. Schleiden and Schwann established that as far back as the nineteenth century. A hundred and fifty years later, Kronkite put forward his theory of cellular weight. As simply as I can put it"—Nine-seven was definitely condescending now—"his hypothesis was that just as different elements have different atomic weights, so different types of cells—cellements, he called them—have different cellular weights."

I shuffled my feet. "But doesn't that deny—"

"It denies all sorts of things. They don't count, so far as this project is concerned. The only part important to us is Kronkite's idea that the weights were subject to change, through metabolism. Complex cellements break down into simple by catabolism, liberating energy. Simple cellements build up to complex by anabolism, using the energy supplied by catabolism or drawn from such outside sources as sunlight."

I threw up my hands. "I fell off. I fell off a long way back."

Nine-seven laughed. His condescension was thick enough to slice. "Most laymen would."

"But what are you trying to do?"

"I thought you'd guessed." Nine-seven checked indicators. "I'm duplicating Aneido."

"You're . . . duplicating . . . Aneido?"

"That's correct." He indicated the seven-foot tank. "In there."

I looked at the tank. Then I looked at Nine-seven. Then I looked back at the tank again. Then I went over to the bed and sat down.

"Kronkite's theory is the key," Nine-seven explained. "Once you isolate your basic cellements, you can metabolize them according to any predetermined pattern by electrosynthesis. This special cymograph"—he nodded to it—"charts cell structures electronically. When we put Aneido in here"—he tapped the matrix chamber—"he became our pattern. And even though the human body is made up of more than a million million cells, the protoplasmic synthesizers—those small tanks connected to the large one—are evolving a twin of him in the Q-tank at this moment."

"And his mind?" I queried.

"The mind's patterns are set by experiences and conditionings," Nine-seven declared flatly. "Van Wagnen conducted a series of experiments in 2004 that proved that all perceptions —that is, all outside stimuli an organism becomes aware of— have a physiological effect. Everything that happens to a person speeds or retards the metabolism of the cellular structures in the various affected areas of the brain and nervous system." He paused and eyed me. "Do you follow me?"

I shook my head. "No. But go on anyhow. It all sounds very impressive."

Nine-seven scowled and his lips drew thin. He worked for a moment at the matrix chamber's dials, then straightened. "I'm merely saying that perception is individual. Once a metabolic pattern is set up in your brain structure—whether it's by an outside stimulus or by Process Q—your understanding and mental processes depend more on the cells and their relationship to each other than they do on your actually having undergone specific experiences."

I nodded slowly, but Nine-seven apparently wasn't pleased with my expression. He said, "You can check what I'm saying by the work the neurologists did with the Rahm stimulator back around the middle of the twentieth century. They found that an electrical charge, focused on key points of the cerebral cortex, would produce the same perceptions as actual stimuli taken in through the usual sensory channels. In other words, if you duplicate a man's cell structure with sufficient precision, the facsimile will not only live and breathe; it will have precisely the same capacity, knowledge and background of experience as the man who served as model."

The speech must have winded him. He turned back to his checking of dials and indicators, and readjusted the flow valves of the protoplasmic synthesizers.

I waited for him to look around at me again, then said, "I'm going to surprise you, Nine-seven. I think I *do* understand what you're talking about. The only thing is, what good will it do to produce a copy of the general? One of him's bad enough; why make another?"

Nine-seven leaned back against the Q-tank. "Would it clarify the situation if I told you we're not going to make the duplicate exactly like him?"

"You mean—"

"I mean that since mental processes are a mere matter of metabolic conditioning, we can control our facsimile's outlook. There's a specific thought pattern common to all Mechanists, and antithetical to the FedGov's nonsensical pseudo-democratic notions."

"Then—"

"Yes!" The corners of Nine-seven's mouth pulled up. It was a leer, more than a smile. A tremor of excitement crept into his voice. "By focusing electrical charges on the proper areas in the frontal lobe, we can give our carbon copy the mind of a Mechanist! He'll have Aneido's personality, his background; but his sympathies will be all with us!"

I sat without speaking for a long, long time. The room seemed to close in on me, and the light glinting on the equipment hurt my eyes, and the cables all looked like hangmen's nooses. I hardly heard Nine-seven rattling on:

"Think of it, Mr. Heffner! Think of it! A member of the Society in charge of Security! It's worth all the years of work it's taken. And this is just the first step! We'll replace the FedGov's key men, all of them—the executives, the leaders. It means complete victory—"

I said, "It means the end of the human race."

"What?" Nine-seven reared back as if I'd hit him in the face.

"You heard me! Man's climb up out of the mud stops here. Evolution's a closed chapter, as of this moment."

"Mr. Heffner!"

I kept on talking: "This is what Aneido's been looking for —the thing all the tyrants in history have dreamed of. It's worse than Maurine Burton's projectoscope, even. That just screens deviation and free thought. This stops them before they start."

Nine-seven stood very straight, a bright spot of angry color on each cheek. "I don't think Zero would care for such talk, Mr. Heffner." Pluto's ice-packs were warmer than his voice. "The Society of Mechanists is dedicated to science and progress. The barrier is the FedGov's insistence on catering to the prejudices and emotions of the mob; the authorities' refusal to accept the counsel of superior minds—"

"Quit trying to recruit me," I grunted. I got up off the bed and walked over to the door.

Nine-seven's nostrils quivered. "Zero will hear of it if I don't get your full cooperation, Mr. Heffner!"

I turned on him. "Get on with it! Zero's going to hear plenty—from me—about this whole idea, just as soon as we get to The Center. The quicker we get the job done, the quicker we can go. Besides, it may take me time to pick up Burton. . . ."

CHAPTER X

I KEPT moving the thil glass around and around on the bar in small concentric circles. Each time, the circle got smaller, till finally I was jiggling the glass on a point. Then I'd take a drink and set the glass down and start over again. It was funny, though. The circles always got smaller; they always went in, not out.

Someone put another coin in the musicord. A brassy-voiced female began singing a song with a wailing chorus line about, "There's a woman for ev-ery ma-a-an . . ."

The shifty-eyed weasel next to me at the bar said, "That's what you need, pal. A woman. That thil's gonna get you if you keep swillin' it down so fast. An' I got just the gal for you—a honey, one of those hot little numbers fresh in from Europa. . . ."

The bartender said, "Shut up, you moron. This guy's got troubles." He swabbed away my latest rings. "Another thil, mister?"

I said thickly, "Yeah. Another thil."

The bartender poured more white murder into my glass. "If it's a woman, mister, she ain't worth it. Believe me; I know."

"Like hell you know." I gulped the thil.

"Have it your way," he shrugged. "Only that punk was right. You're takin' this stuff too fast."

He moved off to wait on someone else. I glanced at the clock. The pickup for The Center was due to leave in less than two hours now. I went back over to the voco and tried Maurine's office again, then her apartment. Neither answered.

At the Electro-Neural Testing section at Humanics Research a man's voice said, "Her work cycle's over, sir. You'd better call her home."

"She isn't there."

"Well, you might try Fred Caudel."

I rapped my glass for another thil. The bartender looked at me, then put his bottle back. "No more for you."

I cursed him and went out into the street. There was a voco station at the corner. For the dozenth time, I dialed the number of Maurine's apartment. This trip, a man answered on the second ring.

His voice held a clipped, official note. "Who's calling, please?"

I thumbed down the button and headed for the nearest autotran port. I ran the tracer a block past Maurine's building. A black Security tran stood at the curb. Loiterers were beginning to gather about the building entrance, craning and talking.

I ran the autotran around the corner, got out and walked back. Another Security tran drew to a stop just as I came up. Two Security agents hurried Fred Caudel out of it and into the building. Some of the bolder loiterers followed the three inside, and I drifted in and up the stairs.

The Security men were in Maurine's apartment. The door was open. I could hear Fred Caudel talking.

He said, "Yes, I guess she must be a Mek, all right. Not that I realized it till just now, of course. But when I saw her with that Raines last cycle—"

A woman's voice rose shrilly: "You bet she's a Mek! And so's John Raines, the dog! They've been playing around together for months."

I stepped past the doorway and glanced into the apartment as I went by.

The furious voice belonged to Raines' scrawny secretary.

A Security man clipped, "All right, that's enough. We'll take your statements later. What we want now is this Burton woman. Get out a general order . . ."

I went back down the stairs, made for the nearest voco and called Nine-seven at our secret pickup station.

He sounded tense and angry. "Where are you, Four-four? It's almost time—"

I said, "Burton's in trouble. Someone's turned her in to Security as one of us."

"But she isn't!"

"That didn't stop Security from putting out a general order on her. They claim she's run off with one of our people here, a fat fool named Raines."

"Oh." I could almost hear the wheels turn in Nine-seven's head. "Four-four . . ."

"Yes?"

"Perhaps she has."

"I doubt it."

"But she could have."

"Could she?" I scowled into my voco. "In the first place, she loathes Raines. In the second, I left Raines stashed in an empty cage-tank not too long ago. It was built for a zanat. So far as I know, there's no way he could have gotten out."

"Oh." Nine-seven held another conference with himself. Finally he asked, "What do you propose to do then, Four-four?"

I traced patterns on the voco with my thumbnail. "I've got my orders. Zero said to bring her in. I'm going to do it."

"Four-four . . ." There was a new preciseness about the way Nine-seven said it.

"I'm listening."

"Zero briefed me about your . . . relationship . . . with this Burton woman when he assigned me to come here from the laboratory."

I didn't say anything.

"You're notoriously headstrong, Four-four. Zero told me so."

"He knew it when he assigned me."

"But he didn't know this situation would arise. For us to stay here endangers the entire project."

"I've got my orders."

"Your orders aren't that strict! We can get along without the woman if we have to. This is sheer willfulness on your part—an immature emotional reaction."

"You can call it that."

"But the pickup—"

Maybe it was the thil talking. I said, "To hell with the pickup. And to hell with you, too. Take Aneido and go, if you want to. I've got a job to finish here."

I clicked off the voco and hit the street again. The Security trans were still parked in front of Maurine's apartment.

I took off in the opposite direction. When I came to an autotran, I grabbed it and ran the tracer over a route through
the old port district, down past the place where I'd left
Raines, the *Chamber of Horrors*.

The Ionian quontab was still—or maybe it was "again"—
beating the percussor with its shoulder-hammers. The redhead stood by the doorway, taking admissions and ballyhoo-
ing the exhibits.

I left the autotran and went into a thil-shop across the
street. There was a woman behind the bar there. I ordered a
thil, then jerked my head in the redhead's direction. "Know
her?"

"Her?" The barmaid's eyes were scornful. "Yeah, I know
her."

"Has she got a voco?"

"I guess so."

I leaned on the bar, and twisted a ten-credit note around
my fingers. "She's an old . . . acquaintance . . . of mine," I
confided. "I'd like to play a little joke on her. Would you
help?"

The barmaid eyed the ten-credit note. "What do I have
to do?"

I grinned. "Just call her on the voco. Say, 'Honey, I
thought you ought to know. There's more between your
Fred and that Burton woman than you think there is. I can
see them from here now.'"

"That's all?"

"That's all. When you've said it, just hang up."

The barmaid reached for the ten credits. Her smile belonged on a happy cat. I followed her to the voco, and she
spun the dial.

Across the street, the red-headed woman in the too-tight

jacket stopped in the middle of her spiel. She turned, tilting her head as if listening, then disappeared inside the building. A moment later I heard her voice on the voco.

My barmaid followed the script to the letter. She even added a long, low whistle after she'd said, "I can see them from here now."

We went back to the bar and I had another thil.

Over at the *Chamber of Horrors*, customers began to file out. Then the woman herself reappeared in the doorway, dragged the quontab from its stand and carried it inside, closing the door behind her.

Perhaps three minutes passed. I shifted and rolled my glass between my palms. Abruptly, the *Chamber's* door opened once more. The redhead came out. She wore street clothes now. Locking the door after her, she walked quickly away. I followed.

Her route took us straight to the deserted wastes of the first port. Cutting around ahead of her, I ducked into a ramping scar that gave me a clear view of the whole area. My quarry headed directly for an abandoned loading tower. Hurrying up the ramp, she opened the door at the second level and went in.

Again, there was a waiting period—of seconds, this time, instead of minutes. Then the redhead came out again. She paused uncertainly atop the ramp and looked about, while I cowered in my pit. Finally, with a last nervous glance, she walked down the ramp once more and hurried back toward the *Chamber* neighborhood along the same route by which she'd come.

I waited till she was well out of sight, then climbed the ramp myself. The door at the top wasn't even locked. Pulsator in hand, I slid inside.

It was too dark to see much. Directly in front of me swayed six baleful, luminous eyes. They were so close I could almost have reached out and touched them. I rocked back flat against the wall and kicked the door open. Light streamed in.

The windowless room was long and narrow, hardly more than a hall. A grillwork cage on wheels stood just clear of the door. The six swaying eyes thrust up through the top. They were on stalks, and they belonged to a full-grown Martian dotol. The creature's clawed tentacles, moving like grass streamers in flowing water between the side slats, reached toward me. Fortunately, they couldn't reach far enough.

Beyond the cage was an open space and a sodden, blubbering lump of flesh that was John Raines. Behind him stood a second cage. This one contained a slimy monster I'd never seen before. It had mandibles that looked as if they could tear off a pound of flank steak at a time.

Beyond it, far back against the rear wall, stood Maurine. She didn't say anything. From the hollow horror in her eyes, I doubted that she could.

There was a broken chair in my corner. I prodded it at the dotol. The clawed tentacles hooked into it in a lashing frenzy. I backed out the door, pulling the cage after me, letting the dotol's own tentacles serve as ropes.

Out on the ramp, the cage began to roll. By the time it hit the bottom it was going so fast the wheels hardly touched. Then it turned over, and the latch broke open, and the dotol spilled out. I didn't worry about it; no dotol could last more than a few minutes in full Lunar light.

I went back in after John Raines. He hardly looked human. His face was puffed till I almost had to hunt to find his eyes, and blood was running out from under his nails, indicating his frenzied attempt to tear a hole in the floor. One of the plastic slats in his coat had come through the collar and was gouging his neck raw, but he didn't seem to notice it. I pushed him over against a side wall, out of the way, and turned to the second cage.

Behind me, a voice said, "Keep right on going, Heffner."

I pivoted, not too quickly.

Fred Caudel stood in the doorway. He had a service blaster in his hand.

"That voco call trick was smart, but not smart enough," he said tightly. "Security's right behind me, but I've still got time to pick up my insurance"—his eyes touched Maurine—"and run for it. So just keep backing till that ariskon in the cage can reach you. You, too, Raines!"

Raines' puffed face came up. He looked dazedly at Caudel and began to blubber again.

"Go on! Back up!" Caudel's lean face wasn't handsome any more.

Behind me, the mandibles were clacking. I didn't move.

"You, Raines—"

Raines' face looked like a twisted lump of gray dough. He threw one horrified look at the monstrosity in the cage—and lunged full-tilt at Caudel.

The blaster roared. I could see Raines' body jerk, but his bulk carried him the rest of the distance. He crashed into Caudel. They went sprawling out the door together and rolled down the ramp outside.

They rolled all the way to the dotol's broken cage. The clawed tentacles whipped round them. I snatched up Caudel's fallen blaster and ran down and killed the dotol, though by then it was too late to do any good. Then I went back and killed the thing with the mandibles.

Maurine still stood pressed flat back against the wall. She hadn't even spoken. I slapped her face, hard.

Her hand came up to her cheek in a tremulous, bewildered gesture. She looked at me as if I were an apparition sprung to life that very moment. Then she began to sob, and I had to carry her out.

Down at the bottom of the ramp, I stopped and stripped off Raines' coat with the plastic strips, then headed back into the rabbit-warren tangle of the old port district. We reached the first buildings just as a Security vehicle spun down the street with its siren screaming.

I pulled Maurine into a doorway. She was still sobbing. I held her close, and my throat got hot and dry and tight. I wished I had a shot of thil.

Then we were on our way again, block after block, till at last we stumbled into the Society's secret station. The pickup was still there, and I wished I had a whole bottle.

CHAPTER XI

FOR A long moment I lay motionless on the bed and stared down at my own body.

The careman grinned. "Feel good to get back into your own skin, Mr. Lord?"

"You'll never know." I ran my hands over my bare belly and down my legs.

"I tried to keep you in good condition—enriched flow in the

nutritor, massage every cycle, electrodyne stimulation."

I flexed my muscles. They were smooth and firm, my bones well-fleshed. "I can see. You did a good job."

"Thanks, Mr. Lord." The careman began laying out my clothes. "I hated to wake you, but Zero sent up the orders himself. There's some kind of a meeting. They want you down there just as soon as you can dress and eat."

"I figured it that way." I got up and went into the lightbath and turned the beam to high frequency. It made my whole body pulse and tingle, drove out the last stiffness. I stayed there a long while, relaxing in it.

The careman had gone by the time I got out. I put on the clean clothes and went down to the lift.

The operator nodded politely to me. "Welcome back, Mr. Lord." And then, with his eyes on the board: "You're to have breakfast in one of the private units—B, I believe it is."

"In other words, Zero doesn't want me to talk to anyone till after the meeting. Is that it?"

"I wouldn't know about that, sir." He kept his eyes on the board.

The waiter who took my order in Unit B was polite and noncommittal, too.

I went over to the narrow slot-window and looked out across the dark, bleak ball of astroidal rock we called The Center. The Dekktordi process that gave us our thin artificial atmosphere had pitted the stone with holes and pockmarks. Down by the cave mouth that served as a disguised foot-entrance, glinting worms of energy from the hidden mindshield licked and crawled and darted, probing endlessly for a haven in some human brain.

I cursed.

The waiter came back. I left the window for a table and

chewed my way through toka with grenamere sauce, fresh berskal eggs and bacon.

The squawker blared. "Alan?" It was Zero's voice.

I flipped the switch. "I'm coming down now." I drank the last of my ronhnei coffee, wiped my mouth and headed for the conference room.

It looked more like a court than a meeting. Three members of the Council were present, plus Heffner—in control of his own mind now—and Nine-seven. Their mouths were stiff and set.

Zero sat at the head of the table. He was the only one who nodded to me. "Sit down, Alan." He gestured to the chair beside him.

I said, "I'd rather stand. What's this all about?"

Zero ran his fingers through his short gray hair. "Just a few questions, Alan." His gaunt face was a trifle flushed.

"Questions?" I laughed out loud. "You mean charges, don't you?"

"Now, Alan—"

I gripped the back of a chair. "Don't guff me! You mean charges—charges from people like Heffner, there, that turned me in to Security to save his own skin. Or Nine-seven, or Gervault, or whatever his name is, who flubbed up on Aneido and then screamed bloody murder because I had to use my pulsator on him."

"Alan!"

"Alan, hell!" I smashed my fist into my palm. "I'm sick of this business! When there's a dirty job, or a hard one, I'm the man you yell for. Then, when I play my shots the way I see them, you throw rules at me and tell me I'm stiff-necked and headstrong. Or even human." I glared them down, one after the other. "All right, so I'm headstrong. Sometimes I even forget I'm a Mechanist and act like a man instead. Like this time. I took over the minds of two members, against regulations—and both of them turned out to be traitors, even if one of them is still sitting at this table. I knocked out Aneido—and I brought him in. I tried to get relief from duty for personal reasons—and I carried out every last detail of my assignment, even when it meant twisting a knife in my own belly."

"Please, please—"

"Shut up!" I snarled. "You've got Aneido, you've got Burton, you've got the plastic out of Raines' coat—and that's all you're going to get! Find some other damn' fool to answer your questions!"

I turned on my heel and strode out of the room. Their sputtering, their squalling—I didn't even listen.

But then Zero himself was running down the hall after me. He caught my arm. "Alan—"

I jerked away. "Forget it!"

"No!" He spun me around. "For the love of Terra, Alan, listen! This belligerence—it only gets you into more trouble."

"All right! I'm listening!"

"These accusations, the business about rules—they're nothing. I'll take care of them. The real problem's Aneido."

"Aneido?"

"Yes, Alan." He shook his gray head wearily. "The Burton woman's been checking him with her projectoscope. She gets thought patterns, but they don't make sense. Not in terms of what we know about Aneido."

"Does that matter?" I asked bitterly. "You've put a Mek into his job. That ought to be enough."

Zero's forehead creased. "Gervault told me how you felt about that."

"Did he tell you I said it was the end of all progress and the human race?"

"Yes. And in the wrong hands it could be. But not in ours." He put his arm around my shoulders. "That's why I always stand with you, Alan: because you see things with a clear eye. We need members like you—men who can temper pure science with humility and understanding."

"But you'll still go on using Process Q?"

"It's the tool we've been seeking—the weapon that will carve our path to power."

"So you'll use it."

"Can we throw it away, Alan?" His eyes locked with mine. "Could you, yourself, when you think of all the lives that have been spent, all the years we've worked and planned?"

I didn't answer.

Zero said, "We want you to check the girl's work, Alan. She gave us the specifications for the projectoscope under narconosis, and the technicians who did the work on it say they're sure they're correct. But she's normal now and almost as bitter as you are, and it could be she's trying to work some trick."

"Where is she?"

"Down in Laboratory Ten."

"I'll go check, then. For whatever that's worth."

I started to turn.

Zero gripped my shoulder. "Alan . . ."

I looked at him.

He said, "They're going to be worth it, Alan—all your sacrifices, all your pain. That woman herself will live to thank you and so will generations yet unborn."

I stared down at the knuckles of my clenched fist. "I hope you're right."

"I know I am, Alan. Good luck, now."

He dropped his hand. I strode off down the corridor, took the lift to the foot-entrance level, and walked back past the mind-shield control room to Laboratory Ten.

A technician I knew came out. He scowled and said, "I hope you can make more sense of this than I can, Lord. And those plastic strips you brought in are even worse."

I eyed him. "What do you mean? What's wrong with the plastic?"

"Nothing's wrong with it. That's just the trouble," he snapped. "We've tried every test in the books on it, and we still can't find any reason for it being melded into that coat."

"And no break on Aneido, either?"

"No, not a thing. Myself, I think that female's crazy. Or else Aneido is. For that matter, any more jobs like these and we'll all be trying to crash the shield just for the jolt."

Still scowling, he stalked off down the corridor. I went on into Laboratory Ten.

Maurine was there and Aneido and a guard. Maurine and Aneido sat at an equipment-littered table. They wore the metal projectoscope helmets. Lines of weariness etched Maurine's face, and there were dark circles under her eyes.

She looked up as I entered and saw me. Her hand leaped to her throat and her cheeks blanched.

I said, "It's been a long time, hasn't it, Maurine?"

There was a moment of empty silence. Then, instead of answering, she turned to Aneido. "We'll try it again now, General."

She turned the activator knob . . . to the left.

I said: "Mother."

The image of a smiling, white-haired woman flashed on the screen. It was the same face that had appeared the other time, back there on Luna, when Aneido threw the word at me.

I said, "You must have misunderstood, Maurine. It's the general we're trying to test, not you. Turn the knob *right* next time."

Her fingers twitched. The screen went blank. "*You!*" she whispered. Her eyes were shiny as polished glass.

I nodded. "Yes, I was Fred Caudel for a little while. There's a thing we call a neurotron—a mind control—"

"You'll pardon me," Aneido cut in. "This thing's too hot for comfort, and I see you have personal matters to discuss." He lifted off the projectoscope helmet, set it on the table and walked over to the nearest slot-window. His heavy face was blank, impassive.

I sat down in his chair. "Maurine . . ."

In a low, tense voice she said, "I loathe you, Alan Lord. I loathe you more than I thought it was possible for me to loathe any man. Down through the years, so long, I'd hoped and dreamed—and now, you've done this to me."

Her fingers twisted at the fabric of her jacket, till the fibers gave and the whole meld ripped.

I caught her hand. "Please, Maurine!"

She just stared at me. It was worse than if she'd jerked away.

I said quickly, "Maurine, it doesn't have to be this way. The Society will control the whole system in another year: every satellite, every planet—even the FedGov. There'll be an end to Security's tyranny. Science will rule. We can be together, happy—"

"Happy? With you?"

I could taste the vinegar and gall.

" 'Science will rule.' " Her scorn burned like acid. "What

do you Mechanists know of science? Science is only a tool, a means to an end. But you've transformed the means into the end and made a god of it—a paranoid god for frustrated 'superior minds.' You won't accept the human race as it is; you've got to try to force it into your pattern. . . ."

She broke off. Rising, she lifted the metal helmet from her head and set it beside the other on the table; she smoothed the dark coil of her hair.

When she spoke again, her voice was dull and flat: "I loved you once, Alan. I even dreamed that perhaps somewhere, somehow, I could love you again. Now I know better. Because you're really a Mechanist now. You measure everything in terms of power for your Society—life, love, your own destiny. You and your kind, you've forced Security's tyranny on us because it was the only way we could stay free from the worse one you threatened. . . ."

Her voice trailed away.

From the slot-window, Aneido said, "There's another thing you should know, Lord. Not all science is in your hands."

I looked up. "What—"

He strode back to the table. "You Meks aren't the only ones with minds. For example . . ." He lifted one of the helmets, pointed to the cable socket. "You see?"

I frowned and leaned forward. "Do I see what?"

"This!"

His left arm whipped round my head. I caught a blurred glimpse of the helmet hurtling at the guard. Then a great club-fist smashed at me. I sprawled on the floor. Before I could move, Aneido had snatched the guard's blaster.

He said, "We're leaving now. Those plastic strips in Raines' coat have a special molecular structure that serves as the focal element for a new-type finder developed by *our* laboratories. We designed it especially to help us locate your Meks' headquarters. If you'll look out your window, you'll see that it works."

Maurine beside him, he backed out the door. The lock clicked. I ran for the window.

The mind-shield's blue-white tracer charges still crawled and sparkled about the cave-mouth. But now I saw red light, too. Out of the darkness of space, great scarlet globeships of the FedGov fleet were sweeping down. The first loomed like a monstrous crimson ball; it had already landed.

The guard wiped blood from his forehead. "Don't worry. That pair won't get far." He tugged open a locker and pulled down a bolt-rifle.

The door's lock splintered with the first shot. As coolly as if he were on a target range, the guard stepped out into the corridor; he sighted and fired.

A hundred yards away, just short of the outer gate, Aneido jerked round in mid-stride and pitched to the floor. The guard sighted on Maurine.

How long can a split second last? A minute? An hour? A thousand years? I swayed there, while eternity came and went in a single moment. Again I heard Zero's words, the things Maurine had said. All the years gone by, the other struggles—they faded away to mist and shadow.

My belly knotted. Because this was the decision point I'd always turned from. This was the awful ultimate, paralyzing instant when I had to make my choice and take my stand. And it had come too late, too late. The guard's finger already was tightening on the trigger; I could see it now. No matter what I did, there could be no victory. The net had drawn too tight about me. Whether I struck as a man, or stood fast as a Mek, Maurine would die and the human race would fall.

Only thought didn't matter; not really. It never does at a time like that. Logic, self-interest—they desert you. Instinct takes over. Hot blood surges. The road you ride is the man you are.

I lunged and jerked the rifle out of the guard's hands. He staggered, off balance; then he caught himself. His eyes flicked to me—half puzzled, half angry. Then the tension faded. His mouth twisted in a slow, sour grin. "Oh. The woman." And, shrugging: "The shield will get her anyhow."

I smashed his jaw with a stroke of the butt and raced for the shield-room.

The duty man came up out of his chair as I burst in. "What the hell—"

I knocked him down, whirled and fired a bolt straight into the tube-unit.

There was a hissing, a crackling. Circuit breakers clicked. I fired another bolt—into the master switch, this time. The whole broad-bank went dead.

I doubled back into the corridor and ran after Maurine. At the end of the hall, the lead-sheathed gate stood open, a dead guard beside it. I stumbled through and went into the outer cave. Ahead, blaster in hand, Maurine was clambering over the rocks toward the globeship.

Then, beyond Maurine, a flanking port opened. More guards rushed out. One kicked the blaster out of her hand before she could fire. The others lunged for me. . . .

CHAPTER XII

THEY took us straight to Zero's office, a bleak, bare cell without even one window slot. Standing beside Maurine in front of the man who'd been my chief, I could feel the tension hum like a fiddler's plucked E-string. The very air seemed to grow chill. Or maybe that was all inside me.

Then, at a word of command, the guards withdrew. The heavy door thudded dully as it closed behind them, and the three of us were alone.

There was an aching moment of silence. Then Zero said, "I'm sorry, Alan. This time you've gone too far."

"Forget it," I answered thickly. "I made my mistake a long time ago. Twelve years back, the day I joined the Society."

His eyes were piercing. "You really mean that, Alan? It's not just this woman?"

I looked at Maurine. She looked at me. "I mean it," I said.

"But *why*, Alan?" Zero spread his hands in a helpless, uncomprehending gesture. "Why throw it away? You could have had anything. Anything!"

"Anything but the right to make mistakes." I leaned on his desk, my palms flat. "That's the trouble, Zero—the thing no real Mechanist can ever understand. The whole human race has got to have the right to make mistakes. Trial and error is still the only way any species can progress."

"And of course, by your logic, that makes me the villain." He smiled a dry, wry smile. "Next time I'll wear a long black mustache."

I let it lay.

His face sobered. He said, "I had such hopes for you, Alan. Even that you might succeed me. And that could mean something, now that we've got Process Q. Because with it, there's no question but that we'll win."

"Even with those globeships out there?" I couldn't keep the incredulity out of my voice. "Even with our atmosphere being drained away?"

"Of course," Zero shrugged. He flexed a paper knife against the edge of his desk. "You see, Alan, we still have Aneido. Our own Aneido, the one you helped create. As soon as we get through to him, he'll call the globeships back."

"And till then?"

"We can hold out. The Center was designed for defense, you know. This office itself is an independent unit. It would take at least a cycle for anyone to break in. And even then, I'd still have my escape hatch"—he gestured to the trap-like door behind him—"to the surface."

"Then there isn't anything for me to say." I straightened and took Maurine's hand in mine. It was cold as ice.

Zero bent the knife between his hands. "There's a bare chance you might still survive this crisis, Alan, if you weren't so stubborn—you know my influence with the Council. As for the woman"—his lips twisted—"Process Q would give you a reasonable facsimile with a conditioned approach acceptable to the Society."

"You're wasting your time, Zero," I said shortly.

"Then I'm afraid you'll have to face the consequences, Alan." There was a note of real sorrow in Zero's voice, but the sorrow couldn't hide the steel. He laid down the paper knife. "The sentence is death. For both of you."

Maurine's fingers tightened on mine. That was all.

My stomach was swirling. The whole scene suddenly

seemed somehow strange and unreal. The thought of death
—that didn't shake me; I'd faced it too many times before.
But to die for nothing, to go down knowing that the Society
still would triumph because I'd helped to bring life to a Mek
Aneido—

Maurine whispered, "It's all right, Alan."

Maurine, who would die beside me . . . I choked.

Zero's bony forehead furrowed. He pressed a button.

The door opened. A guard said, "Yes, sir?"

"Take them away," Zero said. And then, as the guard
stepped forward: "Wait. . . ." He bent across the desk and
snapped on the squawker. "Have we gotten through to
Aneido yet?"

The squawker crackled. "No, sir. But there's something
else—a call from the globeships."

"Put it on my circuit."

"Yes, sir."

The squawker clicked. A deep voice said, "This is Aneido
talking, Zero."

Zero's paper knife scraped the desk. I put my arm around
Maurine.

The deep voice said, "I'm calling on you to surrender."

Zero thrust aside the knife. He leaned close to the squawker grill. "Aneido! You don't understand! This is Zero!"

The deep voice laughed, a short, harsh laugh. "And this
is Aneido, Zero—General Kurt Aneido, not your cheap Mek
imitation!"

I could feel Maurine stiffen against me. Beside us, the
guard sucked in a shocked breath.

Zero's gaunt hand clawed the desk. "You're crazy! Aneido's dead!"

The squawker blared raucous mirth. "Did you take me for

an utter fool, Zero?" the deep voice jeered. "Did you think I'd risk my own neck in your trap, back there on Luna?" The harsh laugh rang louder, longer. "No, Zero! I'm not that raw and guileless. I sent a double, a human double! Whatever you did, you did to him. I'm making a present of the creature you left behind in place of him to our psych lab."

For the fraction of a second the silence echoed. Maurine, Zero, the guard—they stood like living statues.

I knew what I had to do, then. Not for me; it was too late for that. But at least, Maurine might live.

Heart pounding, belly writhing, I fell back one quick step. It broke the guard's paralysis. He started to spin. I kicked for the back of his knees. They hinged. He lurched to one side, flailing wildly, and I chopped a stiff-edged hand down on the back of his neck with all my might.

His teeth clicked together; his head snapped forward.

I leaped across him as he fell. "Maurine!" I shouted. "The door!"

Zero was already surging up from the desk, his face a gaunt, hewn caricature in gray and purple. The paper knife glinted in his hand. "Damn you, Alan—"

I hit him. He went back down in his seat again. The knife rattled on the floor.

I pivoted. "Maurine . . ."

She turned from the closed door. "Don't worry. I've thrown the bolt."

"Good," I nodded. I even tried to mean it. "You'll be safe here till Aneido can get to the escape hatch."

It must have been the way I said it. She stared at me, her face suddenly shadowed. "And . . . you?"

I laughed, after a fashion. "Do I have a choice? I'll wait here with you—till the FedGov hangs me."

Her lovely face went stiff and white. "Alan—"

"Face facts," I shrugged wearily. "To the FedGov, I'm still Alan Lord, Mek agent. Last-minute reformations not accepted. So . . . I wait till I hang."

Beside me, the squawker did things to a deep bass chuckle. Aneido's voice rasped, "That may be a while, Lord, if you've really got Zero penned up with you. Under the circumstances, and from what I've just heard over this circuit, I'll trade you for him any day with no questions asked. All I ask is five minutes to get there!"

The squawk-box clicked off, then, but I still stood staring at it, caught fast in the grip of a creeping, sweeping numbness. There were so many things that surged inside me— shock, sheer disbelief, a hundred others. I was hot and cold at once, both stiff and shaking. I wanted to curse, to laugh, to shout, to sob.

Only I didn't give way to any of them, because then— suddenly, incredibly—Maurine was close beside me, so very close. Her eyes were shining. We didn't mind the wait . . . together.